GULLIVER'S TRAVELS

MOVIE NOVELIZATION

adapted by Sarah Willson
based on the screenplay by
Joe Stillman and Nicholas Stoller

SIMON SPOTLIGHT
New York London Toronto Sydney

SIMON SPOTLIGHT
An imprint of Simon & Schuster Children's Publishing Division
1230 Avenue of the Americas, New York, New York 10020
© 2010 Twentieth Century Fox Film Corporation. All rights reserved. Movie photography © 2010 Twentieth Century Fox Film Corporation. All rights reserved. © 2010 istockpohoto/Thinkstock © 2010 Hemera/Thinkstock. All rights reserved, including the right of reproduction in whole or in part in any form. SIMON SPOTLIGHT and colophon are registered trademarks of Simon & Schuster, Inc. For information about special discounts for bulk purchases, please contact Simon & Schuster Special Sales at 1-866-506-1949 or business@simonandschuster.com.
Manufactured in the United States of America 1010 OFF
First Edition 10 9 8 7 6 5 4 3 2 1
ISBN 978-1-4424-0904-0
ISBN 978-1-4424-0982-8 (eBook)

# Chapter 1

BZZZZ! BZZZZ! BZZZZ! BZZZZ!

An arm emerged from beneath the covers. A hand groped for the alarm. *Bap, bap, bap . . . SLAM!* The alarm stopped buzzing.

Lemuel Gulliver sat up groggily and immediately banged his funny bone against the wall of his tiny sleeping nook.

"Ow!" He rubbed his elbow, but he was awake now. Swinging his legs around the side of the bed, he shuffled into his little bathroom and turned on the drippy shower faucet.

Moments later, dressed in a dubiously clean T-shirt and wrinkly pants, Gulliver sat down at his small kitchen table and opened the morning paper, the *New York Tribune*. He turned directly to the travel section and stared at a small picture at the top of the page. There she was: Darcy Silverman.

Darcy had her own column: "Darcy Silverman's Out and About." She'd written today's column about her trip to Mumbai. Gulliver had never been to Mumbai. In fact, he hadn't really ever traveled anywhere to speak of, but that didn't stop him from reading every word of Darcy's columns. At last he tore his gaze from the pretty, intelligent face in the picture, swilled down the last sip of his bad coffee, slung his *New York Tribune* press badge around his neck, and headed out the door.

Gulliver hurried down the front steps of his shabby apartment building. Out on the street the tall Manhattan skyscrapers towered above him, making him feel small and insignificant—as usual. He trudged into his corner deli to order his breakfast sandwich.

"Hey, Kenny, how ya doin'?" said a burly construction worker standing behind Gulliver.

"Terrific, Mac! What'll it be today?" replied the deli cook. He hadn't noticed Gulliver, who had gotten there first. Gulliver was too short to see over the top of the ordering counter.

"Let me get twenty-eight bacon, egg, and cheese

sandwiches!" said the construction worker.

"Right away, buddy!" said the deli clerk. "That oughtta clean us out of sandwiches for the rest of the morning!"

Gulliver sighed and walked out of the deli with his shoulders slumped.

As he approached the *New York Tribune* building, dozens of people streamed past him, hurrying to get to work. He entered the cool, vaulted lobby, where a large group of reporters, editors, and other professional-looking people clumped in front of the elevators. They all got onto elevators going up. Gulliver stepped into the only elevator heading down.

Later that morning Gulliver sat in his small, airless work area, studying a piece of paper. Behind him was a bulletin board packed with photos, many of them cracked and faded. Across the desk from him sat a young, impatient-looking man.

"Your name's Dan?" asked Gulliver.

"Yeah. Like it says on my resume," he replied drily. "Which you're looking right at."

"What do you hope to get out of working in the mail room?" asked Gulliver, affable as ever.

Dan stared at Gulliver. "What do I hope to get out of working in the mail room? I hope to get out of working in the mail room as soon as possible!"

"You've got sass. I like that," said Gulliver. "You're hired! Welcome to the team." He held up his fist for Dan to bump back with his own fist.

Dan just blinked at him. "I was *already* hired. Not by you, either."

Gulliver leaped up. "First thing we must accomplish today is to—"

"Deliver the mail to the departments that need mail delivered to them?" snapped Dan.

"No! We must document your first day on the job!" Gulliver grabbed Dan and pulled him closer, then took out his iPhone and snapped a picture of the two of them. The printer spat out the photo and Gulliver bounded over to it and tacked the picture up on his bulletin board.

Dan stared at the dozens of pictures. "Wow. How long have you *been* here?"

"Ten years," said Gulliver proudly. He pulled the mail cart out from where it had been stashed and patted it affectionately. "All the great thinkers started out in the mail room," he added.

Dan stared at Gulliver in disbelief.

"If this noble steed could talk, can you imagine the places she has been?" asked Gulliver.

"Up and down the hallways of the *New York Tribune*?"

"Exactly!" said Gulliver. "Now . . . let's go deliver some mail!"

As Gulliver and Dan pushed the cart through the bustling corridors, Gulliver tossed piles of mail into various offices and toward different desks with pizzazz—behind-the-back passes, layups, alley-oops. Unfortunately the mail missed its targets more often than not, sailing over in-boxes, even hitting an assistant in the side of the head.

"Sorry!" shouted Gulliver cheerfully as he turned a corner . . . and stopped outside the office of a powerful editor.

Gulliver tiptoed quietly into the office and placed the pile of mail on the corner of the polished desk. "Your mail, sir," he said deferentially, and began walking backward out the door.

"Hey!" said Dan, addressing the editor behind the desk. "You're Harold Jones, right?"

Gulliver's mouth fell open at Dan's boldness.

"Why, yes," said the editor, looking over the top of his glasses to address Dan.

"I just want to say that I loved your piece on the failure of the derivative market. Terrific stuff," said Dan.

"Well, thanks very much," said the editor.

Dan thrust out his hand. "Dan Quint. New mail guy."

The editor stood up and shook Dan's hand. "I look forward to seeing you around," he said with a smile.

Gulliver seemed to have lost the power of speech during this whole exchange, but as soon as he and Dan had rounded the next corner, he pulled Dan aside.

"What are you doing, man?" he whispered. "Mail room guys are not on the same level as these people! We're the *little people*!"

"I don't want to be one of the little people," said Dan, looking scornfully at Gulliver.

"Who does? Hey, I've got some plans of my own too. Done some writing samples over the years and stuff. But you can't talk to these people like that; you have to respect their work space."

"You're just scared of them," Dan said.

"Nah, it's not like that," said Gulliver as they continued around the next corner. "It's just that . . ." He gulped on his words, then suddenly stopped short. Dan followed Gulliver's gaze.

A pretty, intelligent-looking woman was leaning over her desk. A halo of fluorescent light bathed her in an ethereal glow. She stood back up and faced the other person in her office, a handsome, craggy-looking man wearing an interesting overcoat that clearly came from some exotic place far away.

"Thank you for considering me for the travel writing position," the man was saying. He had an unusual accent, perhaps Australian. "I hope you enjoy these sample articles I've done. If you have any trouble reaching me, it may be because I'm in the midst of ascending one of the higher peaks in the Himalayas." He smiled broadly, flashing bright white teeth.

"Thanks, Nigel," said the woman. It was Darcy Silverman, the travel columnist. "As soon as I've made a decision I will let you know."

As the man brushed past the mail cart without a glance, Darcy smiled at Gulliver. "Hey, Lemuel. Got any mail for me?"

Gulliver stammered something unintelligible, then started fumbling through the mail cart.

"Hi!" said Dan, bounding forward to shake

Darcy's hand. "I'm Dan from the mail room. I'll do whatever it takes to not be from the mail room!"

"Dan's just kidding," said Gulliver, who had finally found his voice. But it came out in a high, nervous squeak. "And he doesn't mean to bother you."

"He's not bothering me." Darcy laughed. "Nice to meet you, Dan. I'll see you guys later."

As they wheeled away from the travel section offices, Dan smirked at Gulliver. "So how long have you had a debilitating crush on the travel editor?"

"Who? Me? Crush? On Darcy? Nah," said Gulliver. "I mean, maybe she has a crush on me, but . . . hey!"

Dan had grabbed Gulliver's iPhone. Now he scrolled to a photo of Darcy, which Gulliver had taken on the sly one day. "Why don't you just ask her out?" he asked.

Gulliver shrugged. "I can ask her out whenever I want. It's no big deal. It would just take me, like, five seconds. I could do it anytime."

"So do it."

"Next time I see her, I will!" said Gulliver.

The elevator doors opened and they rolled the cart in. Just as the doors were about to close, Darcy stepped in.

"Well! Hello again!" she said.

"Gotta go!" said Dan, and with a big wink at Gulliver, he jumped out just before the doors closed again.

Gulliver found himself alone with Darcy.

"So how's the day going?" asked Darcy brightly.

"You know," muttered Gulliver without looking up from the floor.

"What are you doing this weekend?"

"Bunch of stuff."

"Cool."

"Yeah. Cool," he replied.

"Well, have a good one," said Darcy as the doors opened at the lobby. She stepped out.

As the doors closed Gulliver smacked his forehead. "You idiot!" he said to himself. "Why didn't you just ask her out?"

Suddenly the doors opened again. Darcy stepped in. "I forgot something in my office. You going back up too?"

"Um, yeah. I forgot something too," Gulliver mumbled miserably.

Later that day Gulliver tramped into the mail room and sat down heavily in his battered old chair.

"You chickened out. What a surprise," said Dan.

"I didn't chicken out," said Gulliver. "I'm just . . ."

"Being respectful of her work space." Dan snorted.

"So, hey, you want to go grab some dinner? Shoot some pool?" asked Gulliver, changing the subject.

"No," said Dan.

"Hey, no problem!" said Gulliver. "You want to be all bright-eyed and bushy-tailed for tomorrow so you can impress the boss!"

"You're not my boss anymore. I got promoted."

Gulliver was shocked. "That's impossible! This was your first day."

"Yeah, well, they promoted me," said Dan. "Look. You might as well face it. The reason you didn't ask Darcy out is the same reason you'll never leave the mail room. You talk a big game, but that's just it: talk. You'll never amount to anything." And Dan stood up and walked out.

Gulliver slumped back into his chair.

But after he sat and thought for a while, he grew determined. He would do it! He would ask Darcy out! Before he could change his mind, he took the elevator up to Darcy's floor. He walked down the hall toward the travel section offices, as everyone around him was packing up to go home.

"Oh! Hey, Gulliver!" said Darcy, looking up from her desk. "Did you need something?"

Gulliver swallowed. Then he cleared his throat. He started to say something, then stopped. Then he tried again. "I really enjoyed that article you wrote about Mumbai," he said.

"Thanks," she said, somewhat puzzled. "Are you all right?"

"Yes," he said quickly, his newfound courage failing him all of a sudden. "I just came in for . . ." He looked wildly around her office, then snatched up a piece of paper. "This."

"You want to apply for the travel writing assignment?" she asked. "I had no idea you wrote. Or traveled."

"Oh, yeah, I travel all the time," lied Gulliver.

"Oh, wow. Who knew? Well, bring me some samples in the morning, and we'll see what we can do."

Gulliver smiled weakly, wondering what in the world he had just done.

Chapter 2

Later that night Gulliver's tiny apartment looked even more chaotic than usual. Heaps of papers spilled out of boxes, drawers were left open, and the kitchen table was in a hopeless state of disarray. Gulliver rummaged around the back of his closet and finally found what he'd been looking for—a box from his college days. From its depths he dug out a binder labeled "Gulliver's Travels." He opened it up eagerly and pulled out one of his old travel writing pieces. This would be perfect to give to Darcy!

But as he scanned the essay, his smile faded.

"Who am I kidding?" he said out loud. "This writing stinks."

He closed the binder and tossed it over his shoulder. Then he turned and stared at his laptop, deep in thought. An idea came to him. His smile returned. He hurried over to his creaky old bookcase and scanned the battered volumes. Pulling two from the bottom shelf, he sat down to write.

Tap tap tap clickety-clickety clack. Gulliver's fingers flew over the keyboard, and the words flowed down the screen. Every so often he glanced down at the book that was open in his lap: *Fodor's Guidebook to Mexico.* Now *this* was great travel writing! Certainly better than anything *he* could write. *Tap tap tap clickety-clickety clack.* He continued to copy down the words from the book. Then he put down the *Fodor's* and picked up the other book: *Time Out: Barcelona.*

Tap tap tap clickety-clickety clack.

After several hours of copying text from already-published books, as well as cutting and pasting cool-sounding passages from the Internet, Gulliver printed out his "samples" and then went to bed.

✳   ✳   ✳

"Wow, Gulliver. I'm impressed. I had no idea you were such a good writer!" said Darcy.

It was the next day. Darcy smiled radiantly across her desk at Gulliver. She was so hot, he was thinking to himself, he could hardly look back at her—it was like trying to stare at the sun.

"Well, uh, I don't like to brag about the more literary . . . er, literarian side of me," Gulliver replied shyly.

"These samples are terrific. And you have a knack for changing your style so effortlessly. This piece about Mexico feels really classic, like it came straight out of *Fodor's*. And this piece about Barcelona is all sassy, like I'm reading *Time Out*!"

"Well, I have been dipping the old feather in the proverbial black ink, as they say," said Gulliver, shifting uncomfortably in his chair.

"Well, you're hired for this travel piece," said Darcy. "It's the perfect fluff piece to start you off. There's a guy down in Bermuda who claims he has the secret to the Bermuda Triangle. He's either crazy or he's trying to trick tourists out of their money."

As Darcy prattled on, Gulliver tried to remember what he knew about the Bermuda Triangle. He knew it wasn't a *real* triangle. He vaguely recalled hearing that it was an area of the Atlantic Ocean where ships and planes had mysteriously vanished without a trace. And that it was sort of near Bermuda somewhere. He tried to focus on what Darcy was saying.

"I figure this could be a fun way to explore Bermuda and the smaller islands around it. Everything is arranged. Your contact is waiting for you."

Gulliver nodded, still stunned that he was actually getting a real writing assignment. And from Darcy! She obviously hadn't figured out that his writing samples were copied out of books. Maybe she would never find out!

"You do have boating experience?" Darcy was asking. Before he could answer, she continued, "Oh, of course you do. I forgot you said in your cover letter that you covered the America's Cup yacht race. That's good, because I have to be honest, it was hard to find someone for this assignment. You have to be at sea for three weeks. I thought I was going to have to do it, and I *hate* boats. I get super seasick. So what do you say? It's a small story, but are you up for it?"

Gulliver gulped. "There are no small stories. Only small writers," he said.

The next thing he knew, Gulliver was on an airplane, landing at Bermuda International Airport.

As Gulliver exited the gate, he noticed a young man with a sign that read NEW YORK TRIBUNE. Gulliver approached him. "Are you Old Hank?" he asked dubiously.

The young man grinned. "That's my grandpa. You can call me Young Hank. Come on. I have a car waiting to take us to meet my grandpa. He's the one who knows all about the Bermuda Triangle."

After a harrowing drive along dusty, winding roads in Hank's beat-up old van, they finally pulled into a pocked driveway and entered a low, dark, ram-shackle old bungalow. Gulliver, still a little blinded by the bright sunshine, peered around the dim interior. It appeared to be the office of an old seafarer. Miniature ship models, intricately detailed and finely wrought, hung from the rafters.

"Grandpop!" called Young Hank. "Get out here!"

Gulliver took a small step back as an old, grizzled sailor shuffled into the dim light. He carried a mug that contained a dark brown liquid and peered at Gulliver with what appeared to be his one real eye—the other may have been made of glass. He seemed surprised to have a visitor.

"Hi!" said Gulliver brightly. "I'm from the *New*

York Tribune!" He held out his hand for the old man to shake. The old man ignored it, so Gulliver awkwardly put his hand back down. "Uh, cool ship models." Gulliver gestured toward one on a nearby table. "How'd they make them so teeny-tiny?"

"Don't go near them!" the old man shouted, his face darkening suddenly.

Gulliver froze.

"No *mortal* man could have made such intricate models. What do you want?"

Gulliver gulped. "Well, I've been sent to write about the secret to the Bermuda Triangle, and I understand you know all about it."

The old man dropped his mug, which shattered on the floor, spilling the strong-smelling liquid all over. He wheeled around to face Young Hank. "You called the newspaper, didn't you!" he said reproachfully.

Young Hank shrugged. "Well, it's great free advertising for my scuba diving business. We need the money, Grandpop."

Old Hank scowled, then turned back toward Gulliver. He picked up a moldy old ship's log and tapped it. "In this ledger are coordinates that only I know. If you are foolish enough to go to these coordinates, the mouth of the sea will open . . . wide. I have been there myself. I have looked into the abyss. And I have never been the same since."

Gulliver gulped again, then whispered to Young Hank, "What was he like before?"

Before Young Hank could answer, the old man sank into a creaky chair. "I will never tell anyone the coordinates! Now leave me alone!" And he instantly fell into a deep, snoring sleep.

"Right. Okeydokey," said Young Hank. "You heard what he said. So what say we go find you a boat?"

And not long after that, Gulliver found himself standing next to Young Hank at the docks, examining the very small boat that would take him far, far away from shore.

Chapter 3

"The *Knotfersail*?" asked Gulliver. He eyed the creaky vessel. "I guess someone likes puns."

Young Hank helped Gulliver carry a few supplies on board. Then he guided him over to the boat's ancient navigation panel and flipped it on. He punched a couple of numbers in, then pointed at the tiny triangle that began blinking on the screen. "Couldn't be simpler to navigate this thing," he said heartily. "That triangle? Your boat. That dot? Your destination. All you do is keep heading toward that dot. When you want to return, just flip this knob back, and it'll reverse the direction."

Gulliver nodded, trying to absorb everything Hank was saying to him.

"You need help getting out of the dock?"

"I'm good," said Gulliver. "I just throw the thing in reverse, like this, right?"

BAM! They crashed into a boat behind them.

"Whoops. My bad." Gulliver threw it into forward.

BAM! They crashed into the boat in front of them.

Hank nudged Gulliver gently to one side, then took over the wheel. He helped steer the boat out of the harbor.

"This vessel's a little different from the ones I grew up with," shouted Gulliver over the roar of the engine.

"Whatever!" Hank shouted back. "Good luck, man. This is where I hop off." And with one last wave, Hank hopped nimbly off the boat and onto a rocky outcropping near the entrance to the harbor.

Gulliver chugged out into the open sea. He was on his way.

He watched the harbor grow smaller and smaller behind him. Soon it vanished altogether. Everywhere he looked was sparkling blue ocean and baby-blanket-blue sky. The breeze felt bracing; the air smelled salty and clean. Gulliver checked the navigation panel to be sure he was still heading in the right direction. Then he popped the top of a can of ice-cold soda and sat down to write in his travel notebook.

As you head out on the ocean water toward the Bermuda Triangle, the sun is hot and there's, like, reflections and you get so hungry all you want is a nice, juicy cheeseburger and . . .

"Oh, well," he said, clapping the notebook shut. "Quittin' time." Spotting some old magazines spilling out from a storage area, he pulled one out. It was a computer games magazine. The cover story was entitled ROBOT GAMES. "Cool," Gulliver said, flipping through the pages. "A whole issue devoted to how to build your own robot! It even includes blueprints!" He chuckled, then tossed it aside. The rocking motion of the boat was making him drowsy. Gulliver's eyes drooped and his head lolled back as he fell asleep.

✳   ✳   ✳

All of a sudden he was awakened by a fat drop of water plinking onto his nose. Then one plunked on his cheek, and another, and another. How long had he been asleep? Gulliver opened his eyes slowly, trying to remember where he was, and wondering how it could possibly be raining on his face.

"Oh, right," he mumbled sleepily. "I'm in the middle of the Atlantic Ocean, sailing toward some imaginary spot, enjoying the sun and the fun. . . ." He stopped, looked at the scene in front of him, and scrambled to his feet, suddenly wide-awake. He rubbed his eyes. He would have rubbed them again, but a wave nearly capsized his little boat and he had to cling to the side to keep from going overboard.

Behind him, the sun was still shining. Directly in front of him, the sky had turned an ominous shade of pewter, with enormous black clouds. The rain was now pelting down in sheets. The ocean had changed from sparkly blue to a dark, angry gray.

"Oh no," he croaked. He was heading directly into a giant storm!

Gulliver grabbed the wheel and tried to steer the boat away from the storm, but huge waves topped with angry swirls of white foam swelled and roiled around him, tossing his tiny boat this way and that. He looked at the navigation computer, which was streaming with water. It flickered on and off, on and off.

The boat crested over a giant wave. Objects flew off the table, his chair toppled over and bounced overboard, shelves emptied, glass shattered. Gulliver grabbed a life vest and shrugged it on, clicking it together with shaking hands. He reached for his iPhone and punched in 9-1-1.

A crackly voice said, "This is nine-one-one. What is the emergency and location?"

"I'm lost at sea in a giant storm!" yelled Gulliver. "The location is . . . at sea! In a storm! Somewhere!"

At that moment the phone signal cut out. As Gulliver stared at his phone, the rain stopped and the clouds parted. The waves receded and the water went flat. When he looked up, Gulliver felt a huge sense of relief.

"Wow," he said. "That was a trip. Now, let's see, where am I?" He looked at the navigation computer. The triangle—his boat—was directly over the dot. "Wait. I'm here? I'm *in* the Bermuda Triangle?" And just as he said that, a compass on the dashboard started spinning wildly. A metal spoon lying on the deck zoomed toward the metal railing and stuck to it. More metal objects followed, as though bizarrely magnetized. The three full cans of unopened soda he hadn't drunk popped open, and soda spewed upward in three tall geysers. And then Gulliver felt a strange spray of ocean water behind him. Whirling around, he stared up, up, up at a huge waterspout.

"That cannot be real," he said in amazement.

He looked away, rubbed his eyes, and looked again. But the waterspout was still there, and it was bent over, as though it were alive—and sucked up his entire boat.

"AAAAAAH!" Gulliver yelled, desperately hanging on to the wheel.

Now his boat was sitting atop the waterspout, hundreds of feet above the ocean's surface. And then Gulliver's stomach bottomed out as he felt his boat suddenly plunge downward, straight toward the ocean and then below its very surface. The waterspout had become a whirlpool.

"NOOOOOOOO!" he shrieked as the Knotfersail got sucked down into the spinning waters. Then everything went black.

Chapter 4

Gulliver awoke to the sound of lapping waves. Somewhere a seagull cawed, and sunshine warmed his face. He opened his eyes. He was lying on his back, staring at a deep blue, cloudless sky. He tried to sit up.

But he couldn't move.

"I can't move," he said. "Help. *Help! HEEEEELP!!!* I'm paralyzed from the neck down!" No one came to his rescue. He blinked his eyes frantically. At least he could move his head a little. And he could *feel* things. For example, he could feel something crawling all over himself. "What's crawling on me?" he asked, his voice climbing. "Not fire ants. Please, don't be fire ants!"

Suddenly a very small person entered his field of vision. It was a man—a tiny, tiny man! He was dressed in blue, in a style that seemed military, and he carried a large—for him—megaphone. Before Gulliver could react to what was in front of him, the six-inch-tall man opened up a scroll, raised the megaphone to his lips, and began to read.

"I am General Edward Edwardian, Commander of Lilliput! You are herewith charged with aiding the sworn enemies of Lilliput, the Blefuscians."

"Booooo!" yelled a crowd that Gulliver could not see.

Gulliver remained speechless, frozen with disbelief. The man continued to read.

"You are our prisoner now! We shall present you to our king, King Theodore! What say you, beast?"

Gulliver did not reply. Despite his horror, he felt a wave of adrenaline whoosh through his entire body. With every ounce of strength he possessed, he tore his arms and his legs from what turned out to be hundreds of tiny ropes and stakes and pulleys. Ripping the stakes from the ground, he made dozens of little soldiers, who had been standing along his arms and legs and torso, dive off of him and roll to safety. As Gulliver sat up, trailing ropes and pulleys, Edward leaped off his chest and landed on the beach. Gulliver gathered himself up and stood to his full height. He stared down at the army of small, blue-clad soldiers.

"Oh no," said Gulliver. "Where am I? How did this happen? This must be a dream. This *is* a dream. I'm going to close my eyes and then I'm going to open them and I'll be back home in bed." He closed his eyes.

A voice said, "The beast seems to have fallen asleep while standing."

Gulliver kept his eyes squeezed tightly shut. "This is not happening. I am at home. This is just a dream . . . *OWWWWWW!!!*"

He opened his eyes and looked down to see that Edward had jabbed him in the toe with a spear.

"Take the beast down!" commanded Edward.

All of a sudden Gulliver had to shield himself from a volley of arrows and ropes and grappling hooks. Staggering backward, he tripped and fell . . . and passed out again.

When he opened his eyes this time, he found himself tied to a cart, being wheeled creakily through a dollhouse-sized town square. General Edward had assumed a triumphant conqueror pose, standing on Gulliver's chest, as crowds thronged the street.

Because of the ropes binding him tightly to the cart, Gulliver could only catch a glimpse of the town by darting glances out of the corners of his eyes. He took in an old-fashioned-looking village, tidy and well-maintained, with blue banners flapping from rooftops, and packed with people wearing all different shades of blue. Tiny Lilliputians stared in wonderment as Gulliver's cart passed by. Gulliver saw a father gather his children and hug them close, as though Gulliver were a menacing creature that would attack. A few children darted from the crowd and touched Gulliver quickly before dashing back again, as if they'd dared one another.

People began to chant, growing louder and louder: "Down with Blefuscians! Down with Blefuscians! Down with Blefuscians!"

Then Gulliver heard someone shout "Lift!" and he felt the cart he was on slowly begin to rise at one end. Gears clicked and pulleys squeaked as Gulliver was raised to a near-standing position, still strapped tightly to the cart.

A castle rose up into view, and standing at the castle gates, Gulliver saw a king, a queen, a lovely princess, and a somewhat sullen-looking younger prince, perhaps thirteen or so. A jesterlike servant stood just behind the king, and all of them stared at Gulliver quite as curiously as he was staring back at them. Edward, who had jumped off Gulliver and skipped up the stairs to stand with the royal family, stood glaring at Gulliver with a look of revulsion, as though he were a dead beetle pinned to a card.

The princess spoke first. "Are those restraints necessary?" she asked, sounding concerned.

"They are, my innocent, naive, young love," cooed Edward, suddenly using an icky tone Gulliver hadn't yet heard. "They are necessary to prevent the beast from running rampant and destroying our town along with us!"

"What is this creature?" asked the king.

"A Blefuscian spy, your highness," replied Edward with a low bow.

"How do you know he's a Blefuscian?" the young prince asked.

"He wears the color of our enemy," said Edward. "What else could he be?"

"What if he just happens to be wearing a red shirt?" the prince persisted.

"You have much to learn from General Edward, Prince August," said the king sternly, "if you are to be a great soldier one day."

Prince August kicked at a pillar.

Gulliver found his voice. "Excuse me, but I'm not a Blef-shins. I don't even know what that is. Can someone please tell me where I am?"

The king's jaw dropped open. "It can talk! Jinks, answer it."

Jinks, a servant, stepped forward. "You are in Lilliput! The greatest, grandest land in all the world!"

Edward stepped forward, grandly gesturing toward Gulliver. "This horrible giant is hereby declared the property of the state and of Your Majesty, King Theodore."

The crowd cheered.

"You—spy—shall be sentenced to a life of hard labor," the king said to Gulliver sternly. "The Blefuscians should have thought twice before they sent you!"

"I told you, I'm not a Ble-flush-ton!" insisted Gulliver.

"You think me a fool?" spluttered the king. "From this day forth, you exist only to serve and obey!"

And before he could protest further, Gulliver was wheeled away to prison.

Chapter 5

Screeee! Screeee! Caw! Caw! Caw!

From the dim interior of his prison cell, Gulliver could hear the faint call of gulls outside and glimpse the brilliant blue of the ocean. He was chained to the cave wall with thousands of tiny but very strong metal chains. Was he doomed to be stuck on this strange island forever?

Just then the prison warden yelled, "Mealtime, beast! Eat up! You have a busy day of work ahead of you!" A hatch in the ceiling opened and hay tumbled down to the cave floor in front of Gulliver.

"Hey, listen here!" Gulliver shouted back. "I am getting really tired of being called a beast. I may be a giant but that doesn't mean I don't have feelings! And I don't eat hay!"

Chains rattled from a shadowy corner of Gulliver's cell as a voice noted, "It's not so bad if you mash it up with a little water." He had a cell mate!

A Lilliputian man emerged from the shadows. He was also chained, but Gulliver could see that he was young and broad-shouldered, with a muscular build.

"I am sorry my countrymen call you a beast," the young man said. "I do not think of you as a beast."

"Thanks," said Gulliver. "I'm Gulliver."

"I'm Horatio," said the young man, bowing as best he could despite his chains.

Gulliver shook his head slowly back and forth. "No one is going to believe this story when I get home . . . if I ever get back home."

"Why shouldn't they? One's word is one's bond," said Horatio.

"Not where I come from," replied Gulliver, thinking about all the lies he'd told that had gotten him into this mess. "So, are you the only other prisoner in this prison?"

"Yes," Horatio said, bowing his head ruefully. "I was sent here by the great and glorious General Edward because I looked longingly at his betrothed, Princess Mary."

"That Edward dude put you in jail for hitting on his lady? That's cold," said Gulliver.

"I deserve my fate," said Horatio. "I am just a commoner. I have no right to court a lady of the princess's position. The only way I could do so would be if I were to perform a valiant action, and that is impossible for a commoner to do."

"Hey, don't be so down on yourself," said Gulliver. "You seem like a cool guy."

Horatio shook his head. "General Edward is a great general. He is known far and wide for his bravery in battle. I, on the other hand, am but a blacksmith. I am not worthy of the princess."

Gulliver shrugged, rattling his chains. "If you ask me, that Edward guy seems like kind of a lamebrain."

"A lame . . . *what*?" thundered Edward, stepping out of the shadows. He had just entered the prison and was standing there listening to them. "It is my impression that 'lamebrain' is not a nice expression. If such is the case, you shall be thrown into the stocks!"

"What?" said Gulliver. "Oh no. No, no. Where I come from, 'lamebrain' is, like, the highest praise you can say about someone. It means 'brave and courageous.'"

"Is that the honorable truth?" asked Edward suspiciously.

"Yes. It's the truth. Do I look like a liar?"

Edward seemed pleased. "So I am not just a lamebrain. I am a *big* lamebrain."

"The *biggest*," agreed Gulliver enthusiastically. "Now, how about letting me out of this place?

"No," said Edward sternly. "You will now begin your life of hard labor."

And the next thing Gulliver knew, he had been fitted with a huge, complicated harness attached to a pulley, which was designed to lift large stones. General Edward sat on top of a platform strapped to Gulliver's neck, tugging cords that pulled Gulliver's hair painfully.

"Seize! Up! Place!" commanded Edward, tugging at the cord controls.

"Ow! OW!" said Gulliver as he stooped down to pick up a stone and place it on the wall he was constructing. The wall, when finished, would enclose the whole coastline of Lilliput and would protect it from besieging enemies.

Gulliver worked all morning. "Man, it is hot out here," he muttered, after endless stooping, lifting, placing, and stooping again. The sun was now high in the sky. He mopped his brow with a dirty hand.

"Are you tired of working, beast?" asked Edward. His harsh tone had changed suddenly, to one of false, exaggerated concern. "Would you care for a break?" he asked in the same phony voice.

Gulliver was too weary to notice the false tone in Edward's voice. "A break sounds great!" he said.

And soon he was splashing around happily in the cool surf. He lay back and floated, staring up at the sky dotted with white wispy clouds. "I gotta say, slaving isn't quite as bad as I thought it would be."

But meanwhile, Edward had sent word to the palace, seeking an audience with King Theodore near the shoreline. The king had just arrived.

"Our new defense system is now ready, Your Highness," Edward said to the king. "Allow me to demonstrate." He turned and bellowed through his megaphone toward Gulliver, who was still splashing around happily in the shallow waters of the beach. "Come hither, beast! We have prepared a feast for you!" Edward turned and winked conspiratorially at the king.

"Finally! Food!" said Gulliver, splashing through

the surf and heading toward the beach.

Edward threw a switch marked DEFENSE SYSTEM.

As Gulliver sloshed through the shallow water, a series of buoys rose ominously to the surface just behind him. Beneath the water, mousetraps slammed shut on Gulliver's toes.

"Ow!" yowled Gulliver, hopping up and down and trying to nurse several of his sore toes at the same time.

As Gulliver hopped around howling, Edward droned on about technology to the king. The prince, standing near his father, yawned, looking bored.

"Pay attention!" snapped the king to the prince. "Someday you will be a lieutenant in this army!"

Edward nattered on. "The systems are activated when a counterweight hits the platform," he said, "and if the enemy should reach the beach . . ." He hit a button.

Several dozen spiky metal balls suddenly shot out of cannons and landed on the beach in front of Gulliver, who stared down at them curiously. And then several giant paddles rose from the water behind him and smacked his behind with such force, he fell forward into the sand . . . and onto the spiky balls.

"OWWWWW!" yelled Gulliver.

"Our new defense system, King Theodore," said Edward with a small bow, as several soldiers clapped politely.

Observing these proceedings from far out in the ocean, the Blefuscian king put down his telescope and turned to his first officer. "Their defense system is operational," he said. "We must move in for our attack quietly and with great care."

The first officer nodded and gave the order. An elite group of Blefuscian navy fighters, equipped with underwater gear, lowered themselves silently into the water. They began swimming toward the Lilliputian shoreline.

The Blefuscian king leaned toward his first officer. "The people of Lilliput will be so busy trying to put out the fire, they will neglect to protect their princess," he said with a satisfied smile.

In the fields just outside the city, Gulliver was back at work. Edward stood atop the yoke strapped to

Gulliver's back, forcing him to pull forty plows across the field. Horatio, his ankles chained together, stood next to Edward, fanning him.

Suddenly, from a tall rampart of the castle, an alarm bell began to ring.

"A fire!" cried Horatio.

"Two bells mean a fire," snapped Edward. "One bell means we're under attack."

"There were two bells and then one bell," Horatio pointed out as tactfully as he could. "Perhaps that means a fire *and* an attack?"

"Nice alarm system, *not*," muttered Gulliver.

As the three of them looked, smoke curled from the castle.

"The Blefuscians are attacking the castle!" yelled Edward.

"The princess is in danger of being kidnapped!" Horatio added fervently.

"To the castle, beast!" Edward ordered Gulliver.

Chapter 6

Gulliver raced as fast as he could toward the castle, trying hard not to knock into any buildings or step on anything important. Edward stood on Gulliver's neck harness as though he were a captain at the prow of a ship.

Gulliver, Edward, and Horatio spotted the princess standing on a terrace, with Blefuscian soldiers climbing toward her on ropes. "Why is she just standing there, waiting to be captured?" asked Gulliver. "Shouldn't she run away, or at least try?"

"It is our honorable tradition that upon attack, the princess must present herself to the enemy on the kidnapping deck," said Horatio sadly.

"I shall save you, my darling!" shouted Edward, full of bravado.

He forced Gulliver to kneel, then leaped down. The Blefuscians had nearly reached the princess on her terrace.

"Help, help," said the princess, sounding a little bored. "I fear that I am about to be kidnapped."

"I can help," suggested Gulliver.

Smoke was beginning to pour out of the window behind the princess, trapping her on the balcony.

"We do not need your help, beast! Just stay where you are!" yelled Edward, racing for the stairs.

"He will never get to her in time," said Horatio, staring at the soldiers who were now climbing over the wall of the princess's terrace and unfolding a large net to throw over her. The flames were now licking away at the palace wall behind her. "Please save her!"

"But that dude Edward told me not to," said Gulliver.

"I beg you," beseeched Horatio, his eyes wild with fear. He snapped open the last of the bolts that held the harness on Gulliver, and the harness fell away, freeing Gulliver completely.

Just as the soldiers were about to toss the net over the princess, Gulliver loomed above them. The Blefuscians looked up at him and cowered.

One by one, Gulliver gently plucked the soldiers off the terrace and tossed them into the nearby gold-fish pond. One by one, they crawled out of the muddy pond, staring up at Gulliver in dripping disbelief.

"Retreat! Retreat!" yelled the Blefuscian captain. "The Lilliputians have some sort of giant beast working for them!"

Gulliver put his palm down on the balcony in front of the princess, who stepped onto it. He gently placed her next to Horatio, safe and sound and out of danger from the fire. Then Edward burst onto the balcony.

"Fear not, my darling!" He swaggered. "I shall rescue . . . wait. Where did she go?" He looked around in confusion, panting with exertion.

Then the alarm bells started ringing again. Horatio looked at Gulliver, his eyes wide with fear. "Those bells are telling us that the fire has raged out of control and the king is trapped!"

And sure enough, the fire was now raging through the palace. As Gulliver, Horatio, and the princess hurried around to another part of the palace, they spotted the king and several of his soldiers waving for help from the windows of the king's private study.

Smoke billowed out from behind them. They were indeed trapped!

Members of the castle staff were frantically throwing buckets of water on the flames, but it was clearly no use. The fire had grown much too big.

Edward had now hurried into the palace courtyard and was staring up at the king. "Fear not, Sire. I shall save you!"

A burning beam suddenly landed in front of Edward, causing him to jump backward. He stared at the king with consternation.

Gulliver rolled his eyes at Edward and reached toward the window, trying to get at the king and his soldiers. But before he could get anywhere close to them, he quickly pulled his hand back. "OW! Hot! Too hot!" he said, blowing on his hand.

The king gazed down sadly from the high window. "I fear it is too late. This is it for me. You have all served me honorably. May the kingdom of Lilliput last forever."

"Gulliver, you must help us!" pleaded Horatio. "How can we find a great deal of water quickly, to put out these flames?"

Gulliver stared at the doomed king and his soldiers.

He glanced at the princess, who was frantic with distress. He looked at Horatio's pleading expression. He sighed. "Oh, all right. I do have one idea, but you're not going to like it. Stand back, everyone."

Confused, all the Lilliputians stepped back.

Gulliver groaned and turned away from them before unzipping his pants—and peeing on the fire. Great wisps of steam billowed upward as the flames hissed and died out.

"Eeeww," said a few people.

"Sorry, that was gross." Gulliver apologized as he readjusted his clothing.

"That was *disgusting*!" complained Edward. "And it is also grounds for execution!" He whipped out his sword and turned to the king. But the king's expression was not what Edward expected.

"Our savior!" declared King Theodore.

"Our savior!" the grateful princess echoed.

"Gulliver has saved us!" cheered the crowd.

"Aw, gee, really, it was nothing," said Gulliver modestly, feeling a little less embarrassed.

"On behalf of the citizens of Lilliput," said the king, "I thank you for rescuing my daughter from kidnapping, and for rescuing me from certain death, and for doing so after our army had failed to protect us!" He pointed accusingly at Edward, who scowled. "I hereby welcome you to Lilliput, not as a slave, but as our guest!"

"Sweet!" said Gulliver, happy for the first time since arriving on this strange island.

"We request the honor of your company at a royal banquet this evening," the king continued. "Will you accept?"

Gulliver was about to eagerly accept the invitation when he stopped himself. He looked at Horatio, who was staring at the ground. "I will, on one condition," Gulliver finally replied.

The crowd murmured. The king raised a royal eyebrow. "What is it?" he asked.

"That you also free my friend Horatio here and allow me to bring him to the banquet as my guest."

After a brief moment, the king nodded.

The princess smiled.

Horatio beamed.

Edward scowled again.

Chapter 7

"I have never been to a royal banquet!" gushed Horatio. He and Gulliver were standing just outside the palace gates. "I am forever indebted to you, my sweet, sweet Gulliver."

"That's great," said Gulliver. "But, really, there's no need to call me 'sweet.' Let's try this instead." He put his giant fist right in front of Horatio's face.

Horatio looked up at Gulliver in confusion.

"You pound it. With *your* fist. C'mon, don't leave me hanging."

Horatio reached out with his fist and very tentatively pounded Gulliver's fist with his own.

"Now let's go par-*tay*!" said Gulliver.

The king and queen sat at one end of the long banquet table, which was filled with meats, cheeses, fruits, and other delicacies. Gulliver was ushered in and seated at the other end in a special chair that had been constructed by a team of Lilliputian carpenters. Scores of Lilliputians lined the table on each side, and behind them, ice sculptures dotted the courtyard. One sculpture depicted Gulliver saving the princess. Another showed Gulliver throwing the Blefuscian enemies into the pond. Another reenacted Gulliver putting out the flames of the castle—except that in the ice sculpture, a champagne fountain flowed out from Gulliver.

Horatio was directed to sit down in an empty chair directly opposite the princess and right next to Edward, who was not at all pleased to have Horatio as a dinner table neighbor.

A platter was set down before Gulliver that had six roasted pigs. He ate them in six bites.

Just then a servant accidentally dribbled wine on Edward's sleeve. Edward sprang from his chair, his eyes flashing. "You fool!" he shouted at the cowering servant girl. "You have ruined my coat! I shall have you thrown into the stocks!"

Horatio quickly came to the defense of the servant, even though he had nothing to do with the accident. "It was my fault!" he said. "I accidentally knocked her arm. My deepest apologies to the great and glorious General Edward." Edward glared at Horatio, then hurried away to clean his coat.

Princess Mary, who had seen the whole thing, leaned forward. "Your chivalry has not gone unnoticed, Horatio."

Horatio gasped. "You . . . you know my name?" he said as his face turned bright red.

The princess giggled.

When Edward returned, he made a toast: "To warfare! Our valiant struggle has lasted for five centuries!"

"Which is why my son, the prince, must become a soldier," said the king, "and not an actor."

The prince rolled his eyes.

"What are you guys all fighting over?" Gulliver asked King Theodore.

"Several hundred years ago, the Blefuscians kidnapped our princess," replied the king.

"That's awful. Why'd they do that?"

"Because we had kidnapped *their* princess. But you must understand the grave circumstances."

"What were they?"

"Previously they had kidnapped *our* princess."

"And, let me guess," said Gulliver. "They did that because you guys had just kidnapped *their* princess?"

The king looked impressed.

"You have read the Ancient Histories?" asked Jinks the servant.

The king addressed Gulliver. "Some of my subjects believe you come from the Island Where We Dare Not Go."

At the mention of the island, the crowd hushed. Several people murmured nervously.

"No. I come from the island of Manhattan. What's the Island Where We Dare Not Go?" asked Gulliver.

The king pointed out toward the ocean. "There. Beyond the fog bank."

"Well, I came here on a whirlpool-thingy. But what's *on* the Island Where We Dare Not Go?"

The crowd gasped and started murmuring again.

"We dare not say," replied the king. "Just never go there. What sort of kingdom is Manhattan?"

"Oh, it's not a kingdom. It's a democracy. Every four years we elect a president."

"You are so honorable and courageous, you must surely *be* the president," said the queen.

Before Gulliver could set her straight, the princess scoffed, "Of *course* he's the president, Mother."

"Were you a victorious president?" asked the king.

"And noble as well?" asked the queen.

"Uh, well, sure. Yeah. Victorious and noble, that's me. I was known as President the Awesome."

"Pah!" said Edward. "That sounds unlikely."

"For shame, Edward," said the king. "Why would you doubt him? His word is his bond. To break one's word is a fate worse than death."

Gulliver shifted uncomfortably.

"When will you return to your home, oh noble and awesome President Gulliver?" asked the princess.

"I should think it would be soon, right?" said Edward sarcastically. "They must be falling apart without you, their great hero."

"Well," said Gulliver, "without my boat, I think I'm stuck here."

"Then we shall build you a worthy living place," said the king. "Lilliputians are famous through-out the land for our building skills. We can build *anything*."

"Wow. These guys *can* build anything!" said Gulliver. It was several days later, and he had just awakened in his newly built house. He sat up in his comfortable bed, which the Lilliputians had fashioned out of cowhides. He reached for his travel diary and wrote in it.

It is day seven of my stay on Lilliput and I don't know if anyone else will read this. But in case they do, I probably should write down what I'm seeing. While the newly arrived visitor to Lilliput might be put off by their initial attempts to enslave you, they turn out to be a welcoming bunch and excellent hosts. They also come up with supercool ways to make one feel at home. And they insist on learning about my world, so I'm telling them all about the important stuff, such as my favorite movies (namely, <u>Star Wars</u> and <u>Titanic</u>). The only thing is, they believe these stories are real, and that they happened to me. . . .

After writing several more pages, Gulliver rose from his bed and padded into his luxurious and spacious new bathroom. The shower was a pure, freshwater waterfall that the Lilliputian engineers had managed to redirect by way of complicated aqueducts, and channel into his shiny faucet.

After showering and dressing, he walked into his sparkling kitchen and pulled a lever on a giant steam-powered machine. A large brass crane tipped, pouring coffee into a brass cup.

Parts of Gulliver's Lilliputian dream house were still under construction, but the Lilliputians were fast workers. He walked toward the media room, waving to the dozens of workers hammering and sawing away.

"Good morning, valiant Gulliver! Hail, bravest Gulliver!" they all chorused as he passed by.

Gulliver walked into his media room and flopped down on a comfy couch. A passable imitation of a flat-screen television sat directly in front of him, but instead of recorded dramas, real Lilliputian actors reenacted Gulliver's favorite movies. "This is the life," he said, settling back to watch a show.

The next day Horatio dropped in for a visit and discovered Gulliver watching his "TV." Joining him were several dozen Lilliputian kids and the king and queen, who were all riveted, watching actors reenact *Star Wars*.

"Obi-Wan never told you what happened to your father!" said a Lilliputian Darth Vader.

"He told me enough! He told me you killed him!" said Prince August, playing the role of Gulliver Skywalker.

"No, Gulliver. *I* am your father!"

The crowd gasped, as the court band attempted to play the *Star Wars* theme. The curtain fell and everyone applauded.

"Gulliver," said King Theodore in an admiring tone, "You have lived a thousand lives! Imagine, being president of your land, and being on the *Titanic*, and battling the Galactic Empire. Now I know what you do all day in your kingdom!"

"Uh, well, not *all* day," said Gulliver. "We go outside, too. We play sports and stuff."

"Sports?" asked King Theodore with a puzzled expression.

And that's how Gulliver came to teach the Lilliputians basketball. The king summoned his royal scientists, who reconstructed a basketball court, a net, a backboard, and a ball. Gulliver even taught the courtiers how to trash-talk one another.

Later, Gulliver sat with Horatio near the palace's lake, contemplating all the fun they'd had that day.

"So you invented the game of basketball during your esteemed career in the Great Mail Room?" asked Horatio, his eyes wide with admiration.

"Yeah, a lot of my inspiration came from there," said Gulliver. Then he quickly changed the subject. "So I saw you make a little eye contact with the princess. How's that going?"

Horatio smiled. "I think, if all goes well, within two or three years she might actually deign to speak to me."

"Hold on," said Gulliver. "You gotta shoot higher than that. To land a princess, you gotta employ some grade-A courtage!"

"Is that how you wooed your princess?" asked Horatio.

"Yeah, of course," said Gulliver.

"What is the name of your princess?"

"Darcy Silverman."

"What land does she rule?"

"Manhattan. Check her out." Gulliver turned

on his iPhone, which was able to display pictures although there was no phone signal. He showed Horatio the picture of Darcy.

"She has the radiance of a thousand suns," said Horatio. "Oh, Gulliver, will you teach me to woo Princess Mary as you have wooed Princess Darcy?"

Gulliver grinned and nodded. He stood up, lowered his hand so that Horatio could step onto it, then carefully lifted him up and placed him in his shirt pocket. "Let's go woo a princess," he said.

Chapter 8

Princess Mary stood on the deck outside her chambers, leaning on the balustrade and sighing at the moon.

"Oh, Princess!" whispered a voice from below. It seemed to come from behind a tree, some distance away. "Wherefore art thou, Princess?

"Hello?" said the princess, peering down into the shadowy grounds. "Who calls?"

"It is I, Horatio," he called back.

"Why so far away?"

"What do I tell her?" Horatio muttered out of the side of his mouth to Gulliver, who was hiding behind a tree. "I don't dare get closer or she'll see you here."

"Just tell her you don't want to get caught and make her dad mad," whispered Gulliver.

"I must keep myself hidden, so as not to invoke the ire of your father!" Horatio called to her. He darted a glance at Gulliver. "*Now* what do I say?" he whispered pleadingly.

"Okay," said Gulliver. "Repeat what I say: But I must be honest . . ."

Horatio called to the princess, "But I must be honest . . . ," he said.

"I have come to tell you . . . ," Gulliver prompted.

"I have come to tell you . . . ," Horatio repeated.

Gulliver couldn't think of a thing to say.

"Tell me what, Horatio?" asked the princess, a dreamy look in her eyes.

Gulliver frantically thought of the most romantic words he knew and all he could come up with was the song, "Sweet Adeline."

"Aha!" he muttered. "Sweet Adeline! Sweet . . . *princess mine*! That'll work." Then he told Horatio, "Repeat what I tell you. Say, 'Sweet princess mine . . .'"

Horatio called up to the princess, "Sweet princess mine . . ."

"For you I pine," prompted Gulliver.

"For you I pine," repeated Horatio.

"In all my dreams, your fair face beams."

"In all my dreams," said Horatio, "your fair face beams."

"You're the flower of my heart," said Gulliver.

"You're the flower of my heart," said Horatio.

"Sweet princess mine."

"Sweet princess mine."

"Horatio," said the princess adoringly, "these passionate words could get us in trouble. Yet, what beauty emanates from your lips!" She put a hand over her heart. Then she jumped. "I hear someone coming! Until the morrow!"

She rushed inside.

Gulliver and Horatio exchanged a fist bump.

When Princess Mary entered her chamber, she found Edward staring at her.

"To whom were you speaking, my darling?" he asked, baring his teeth in an attempt to smile.

"No one," the princess replied. "I was just thinking about flowers. And, uh, pines," she replied. "What are you doing in my chamber?"

"I have come to court you, as I always do at this time of day. Or have you already forgotten who is your one true and eternal love?"

"Oh, right," said the princess. "Is it that time

already? Sorry, I was playing foosball this afternoon with the giant, and I lost track of time."

Edward frowned. "I do not trust this beast. Being a woman, you are too simple and innocent to be a good judge of character."

This time the princess frowned. "Whatever you say, Edward," she said.

Chapter 9

The princess and Horatio went for a walk the next evening. They strolled along the beach, which was bathed in silvery moonlight. They bought snacks at the boardwalk, ate and chatted, and grew more and more comfortable in each other's company.

They passed Gulliver, who was standing with his notebook, writing away, waiting for his dinner order. They waved up at him as they strolled along.

"Gulliver, your twenty-eight bacon, egg, and cheese sandwiches are ready!" shouted the Lilliputian deli clerk. Gulliver grinned and thanked him, then wrote more in his journal:

I am beginning to love this place more than my own home.

* * *

Meanwhile, Edward was also walking along the beach, beyond the outskirts of the town, all by himself. But he was not enjoying the beautiful moonlight, nor was he thinking about how much he loved Lilliput. He was plotting how to get rid of Gulliver. As he trudged along, thinking dastardly thoughts, he suddenly stumbled over something half buried in the sand. He tugged it free and brushed away the sand and seaweed. It was a computer magazine, the one Gulliver had found on the *Knotfersail.* The pages fluttered in a sudden breeze, and he saw that it included detailed instructions on building a robot. And then Edward saw something just a bit farther down the beach—the *Knotfersail* herself! She was half submerged in a tidal pool, but the boat appeared to be more or less in one piece.

Edward hurried off to round up an army of carpenters. He could soon be free of the beast!

* * *

Ding-dong! It was the next day, and Gulliver skipped through his clean, airy house to answer the doorbell. It was Edward, and for once he was smiling.

"I have good news for you," said Edward. "I have discovered your boat. So now you may finally return from where you came. Immediately, if not sooner."

"Uh, wow!" said Gulliver, trying to absorb the sudden news. "Lead me to it!"

Edward directed Gulliver to the port where the *Knotfersail* was docked. Then he hurried off to spread the news that Gulliver would soon be leaving.

It didn't take Gulliver long to walk to the port. He approached his old boat and stared in amazement. The Lilliputian carpenters had put it back together in perfect condition. He really *could* leave!

"Why do you look so forlorn, noble protector?" Gulliver heard a voice ask.

He turned. It was the princess, sitting by herself near the waterfront. He knelt down to speak with her.

"Me? Forlorn? Nah."

"Well, *I* am forlorn," said the princess. "I don't know what to do. I think I'm in love with Horatio."

"That's awesome!" said Gulliver.

"It is not awesome. It is a disaster. Horatio is a lowly commoner. I am a noble princess. Yet when I am near him, my heart flutters."

"Well, that's nothing to be forlorn about," said

Gulliver. "Most people live their whole lives and never feel that way. Follow your heart."

"But my heart is promised to General Edward. If I break that vow, he will lose honor and respect. He will die of a broken heart!"

"He's exaggerating. All guys say stuff like that."

The princess laughed. "I will miss you, fair Gulliver. But why are you still looking so sad? Don't you want to go home?"

Gulliver sighed. "Well, I guess I was just starting to get used to this place, is all."

"But don't you miss your subjects? And the White House? And the *Millennium Falcon*? And your princess, Darcy?"

Gulliver flinched uneasily. Had he really told all those lies? "Well, uh, truth is, Princess Darcy and I aren't super close."

"That's because you are so far away. How will you get closer if you stay here?"

Princess Mary was right, Gulliver thought. He would return home.

Lemuel Gulliver had always felt small in the big city, and was always at a loss for words when he bumped into his crush, Darcy, at work.

Wanting to impress Darcy, Gulliver worked hard
on his writing samples – and Darcy rewarded
him with a travel assignment!

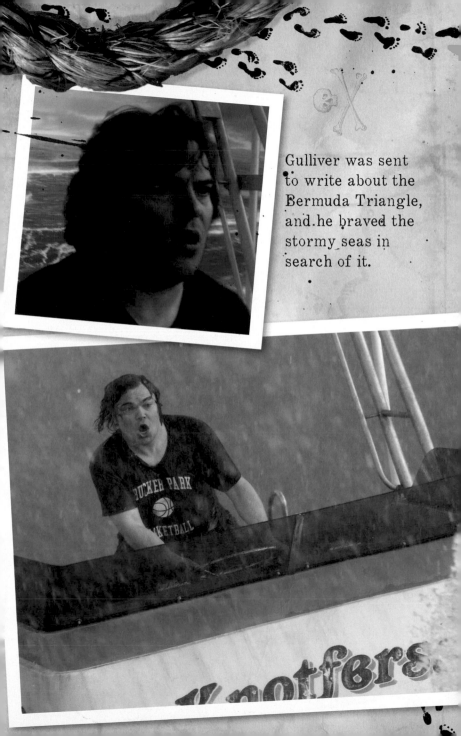

Gulliver was sent to write about the Bermuda Triangle, and he braved the stormy seas in search of it.

Waking up after being tossed off the boat, Gulliver found himself captured – by really tiny people!

Chapter 10

Gulliver waved good-bye to the cheering crowds of Lilliputians lining the beach. The *Knotfersail* was still docked, but in just a few minutes he would be on his way. A banner across the harbor read FAREWELL, OUR GLORIOUS PROTECTOR! Below the banner, a huge golden basketball—of a size that would be the equivalent of a basketball a human might use—was mounted atop the wall, to commemorate Gulliver's introduction of that great game to the Lilliputians. The king's band played a stately tune.

Gulliver kneeled to say a last good-bye to his friend Horatio, who was standing on a dock near where the *Knotfersail* was tied up.

"I shall think of you often and always, fair and gentle Gulliver," said Horatio.

"You too, Horayshe," replied Gulliver, dabbing at the corners of his eyes.

They bumped fists.

The king mounted his podium and addressed the crowd. "Honest Gulliver, who never lies and whose word is his bond, we Lilliputians would like to thank you for being our fair and honorable protector! We wish you a safe passage!"

The crowd cheered. Gulliver waved. Then he turned on the navigational computer and flipped the reverse direction knob. With one last wave at the receding island and diminishing sounds of cheering, Gulliver turned his back on Lilliput and faced forward. After a while, he sat back in his chair and basked in the warm sunshine.

Gulliver was later awakened from a peaceful doze by a spray of cool water in his face. He opened his eyes to behold the giant whirlpool. His little boat was nearly at the edge of it. He scrambled to his feet and clutched at the railing, trying to peer into the swirling depths.

Beep! Beep!

Could it be? Gulliver pulled out his iPhone and stared at the screen in disbelief. He had phone service!

And he had at least a dozen voice-mail messages!

Forgetting the whirlpool for the moment, Gulliver hit the first voice-mail message and listened.

"Hey, Gulliver." (It was Darcy!) *"It's Darcy. I just realized why I felt like your writing came straight out of the* Fodor's *travel guides. BECAUSE IT DOES! Call me back as soon as you get this."*

Gulliver blanched. His mouth went dry. The *Knotfersail* was teetering at the edge of the whirlpool. He checked the next message.

"Lemuel. It's Darcy again. Call me. I mean it. Running away from this is not going to help."

He checked the next one.

"Darcy again. Because you lied to me about being a real writer and are actually a plagiarist and now won't call me back, I have to do your stupid assignment, get on a boat, and throw up for three weeks. So thank you for that!"

Gulliver shoved the phone back into his pocket. His boat was beginning to move in a circle, just at the brink of the whirlpool. What should he do now? It was decision time.

"All right, Gulliver," he said out loud, above the noise of the rushing waters. "You can either man up and go back to Manhattan and face Darcy and tell her the truth, or you can just be a miserable coward and run away, back to Lilliput. Which is it going to be?"

It took Gulliver roughly one second to make his decision.

He raced to the navigation panel and flipped the reverse direction knob.

Chapter 11

Gulliver stood on the deck of the *Knotfersail*, which was now once again moored at the Lilliput harbor.

He waved to the crowds that had gathered to welcome him home. A large banner read WELCOME BACK, OUR GLORIOUS PROTECTOR! The royal band played a welcome home number. Horatio, the princess, and the rest of the royal family cheered wildly. Some people in the crowd actually wept with joy at his return. The only one who looked decidedly unhappy was Edward.

"I promise never to leave you guys again!" shouted Gulliver. "I'm here to stay forever!"

The king felt a tug at his sleeve. Turning, he saw that it was Edward, requesting permission to whisper in the royal ear. Obligingly, the king leaned toward Edward.

"Noble and valiant King Theodore, may I speak frankly?" whispered Edward.

"Yes, what is it?" the king replied.

"If I may be so bold to say . . . I trust not this Gulliver beast who has returned to our midst."

"Well, I disagree," snapped the king. "I think your job is stressing you out, Edward. I think you should take some time off. Relax a little."

Edward's eyes widened. "But, sire, I am Lilliput's most honored military commander! Not to mention the greatest lamebrain in all the land! Who would run our army if I were to take time off?"

The king looked thoughtful.

"Gulliver!" shouted the king.

Gulliver turned toward the king and bowed awkwardly. The crowd fell silent. The band ceased to play.

"I would like to introduce our new commanding general! General Gulliver, you are now the leader of the Lilliputian army!" The king gestured to some soldiers standing nearby, and they immediately sent a soldier up to pin a medal onto Gulliver's shirt, using a complex assortment of ropes, cables, and pulleys. The king continued, "Edward is now the vice general until further notice."

The crowd roared with approval.

"Uh, gee, thanks, Your Highness," replied Gulliver. "I look forward to working with you." His smile broadened mischievously as he turned to Edward. "And to working with *you*, Vice General Edward."

Edward bowed stiffly, his face purple with rage.

When the crowd finally stopped cheering, Edward slipped quietly away.

✳   ✳   ✳

"You are relieved!" Edward told the two guards. He had entered the guard station where two Lilliputian soldiers stood on either side of the Defense Initiative Lever.

"Uh, thank you, Vice General Edward," said one of them. Both looked surprised to see him there.

Edward winced slightly at being addressed as "Vice General," but he recovered quickly. Sternly he saluted the two guards and then watched them depart. He looked up and down the beach, but no one else was visible. He was alone in the guard station. He strode over to the lever and switched it from on to off. Then he pulled a large rock from his pocket and smashed the lever, breaking it completely.

"Now the defense shield is forever off!" He cackled. "Let's see how you deal with that, *General* Gulliver!"

Far offshore, the Blefuscian sentry ship bobbed up and down quietly in the swells. A Blefuscian sentry peered through his binoculars at the Lilliputian harbor. As he watched, the Lilliputian Defense Initiative catapults retracted and disappeared. He blinked and looked again, then turned to the Blefuscian king.

"Sire," he said, "The Lilliputians appear to have turned off their defense system."

The king raised an eyebrow. "Well then, prepare to attack."

Chapter 12

Ding! Ding! Ding! Ding!

Horatio dashed into Gulliver's house and skidded to a stop in front of Gulliver, who was lounging in his media room. "The Blefuscians are attacking!" he cried.

"Are you sure?" asked Gulliver, sitting up and listening to the alarm bells.

"Yes!" said Horatio. "Which means they will attempt to kidnap the princess again!"

"Let's roll," said Gulliver. He held out a palm for Horatio to hop onto, then slipped him into the pocket of his shirt and headed for the castle.

"What's going on here?" asked Gulliver a few minutes later as he approached Edward, King Theodore, and the rest of the Lilliputian troops. A few soldiers were still scrambling out of their barracks, preparing for battle. Out on the harbor, dozens of Blefuscian warships had appeared on the horizon, and were zooming toward Lilliput.

"Oh, finally, our brave general has arrived," said Edward in a flat, unemotional voice. "The defense system has failed. We will never get to our ships in time." There was a malicious sparkle in his eyes. "Brave Gulliver, as our *general*"—he spat out the word—"you must lead the army to save Lilliput and vanquish the entire Blefuscian armada."

"You want me to vanquish all of them?"

"Yes."

Gulliver set Horatio down gently and stood back up, peering at the dozens of warships that were fast approaching.

"The princess will surely be kidnapped this time!" wailed Horatio.

"No she won't," Gulliver said firmly. "I've vanquished before, I can vanquish again."

"Thank you, fair Gulliver!" called King Theodore as Gulliver splashed into the water.

When Gulliver reached the group of ships, he addressed the best dressed of the Blefuscians, whom he assumed was the king. "Hey, dude. I come in peace. The Lilliputians want me to vanquish you guys, but I don't want to turn this into a big ugly battle. Why don't you all just . . ."

"FIRE!" yelled the well-dressed Blefuscian leader, who was, in fact, the king.

Hundreds of miniature cannonballs shot from hundreds of miniature cannons, slamming into Gulliver's legs, arms, and torso quite painfully. But just as the cannonballs hit Gulliver, they bounced off him and headed back toward the Blefuscian ships, crashing into the vessels and sails. As the horrified Blefuscian soldiers watched, Gulliver calmly stooped down and began gathering up the anchor lines of each ship as though he were picking a bouquet of daisies. Then he pulled the entire fleet out of the harbor and gave it a shove back out toward the open sea.

Back on the Lilliputian shores, the crowd roared with admiration and delight. Gulliver bowed modestly and splashed back to shore.

The next day, King Theodore presented Gulliver to the Lilliputian troops. "All hail our victorious general!" he called.

Gulliver bent down and held out his fist. Fifteen Lilliputian soldiers fist-bumped him back. He stood up again and spoke. "It is my honor, as your great and victorious general, to formally dissolve the armed forces! You guys are free to go home now!"

"What!" thundered Edward, above the cheers from the soldiers. "You cannot do such a thing! The army is as ancient as the nation of Lilliput. Without battle training, what will the army even do?"

"Oh, that's no biggie," said Gulliver cheerfully. "I'm going to teach them to play basketball. And the ones who can play guitar can join the guys at my media center and be guitar heroes. And the ones who are good with swords can give me a haircut. I could use a haircut, actually."

Edward couldn't reply. He was speechless with fury!

Gulliver and Horatio headed back to Gulliver's house to play some Rock Band. As they settled back to play, using live Lilliputian guitar-playing soldiers, Horatio asked Gulliver, "I have been thinking . . . do you think it was wise to disband the army? What if the Blefuscians attack again?"

Gulliver rolled his eyes. "No one's attacking this place. Not with me around. Look at me! I'm a one-man wrecking crew! What's more important," he said, turning to face Horatio squarely, "is what is going on between you and the princess. Like, have you kissed her yet? Or is your relationship about to fall into the friendship lagoon?"

Horatio blushed. "No. No, I have not had the honor of having a kiss bestowed upon me."

"Well, that's why you have to man up and be direct. But not too direct. You can't appear to be too interested. Women like men to be a little standoffish."

"Even a woman as fair and luminous as your Princess Darcy?"

"Oh, uh, sure. Even Darcy." Gulliver put his hands behind his head and leaned back. "In the early stages of our relationship, she would get on the elevator with me and I would literally say nothing. And it would drive her crazy. But in a good way."

Horatio furrowed his brow. "That does not seem logical," he said uncertainly.

"There's nothing logical about love."

"Thank you, Gulliver," said Horatio. "I don't know what I would do without your deep knowledge of amorous relationships. Next time I see the princess, I will try out this new technique of speaking standoffishly."

"Go for it, man," said Gulliver heartily, and the two fist-bumped.

✳ ✳ ✳

The princess was in her chamber. There was a knock at her door. She flew to it and opened it, an expectant look on her face. But it was only her brother, Prince August. "Oh, hi," she said with a sigh.

Oblivious to her disappointment, Prince August bounded in excitedly. "Playing the role of Gulliver on his wide-screen television stage has made me sure that my true calling is to be an actor!"

"Wow, um, that's wonderful," said the princess.

"Father doesn't think so," said Prince August, his face turning glum.

"You know what Gulliver would say?" said the princess. "Follow your heart. Your only duty is to yourself."

Just then they both heard footsteps, and Prince August turned to see Edward at the door. The prince turned back to his sister. "Is that what *you* are doing?" he asked reproachfully. "Following your heart?" Then he walked out, barely nodding at Edward as he slid past him.

Edward did not wait to be invited in. He entered

the chamber and plopped down on a couch, propping an ankle up on one knee and leaning back comfortably as though he owned the place.

"What are you doing in my chamber?" the princess asked coldly.

"I have come to court you as I always do at this time of the day."

"Well, I am not in the mood to be courted right now," she said irritably. "I have a headache."

"I can court you when I wish to court you!" Edward snapped back. "It is your womanly duty!"

The princess glared at him. "I am not sure how I feel about you, Edward."

His jaw dropped. "But we are to be married! You are to be my bride!"

She crossed her arms and lowered her chin. "I don't believe we love each other. I'm just not that into you. Can we be friends?"

He leaped up. He could not believe what he was hearing. "You cannot break our engagement! This is a fate worse than death!"

"Oh, pshaw," scoffed the princess. "You're just being melodramatic. Gulliver warned me that you would act like a baby."

Edward's face went red with anger. "You shall be sorry you ever crossed General Edward," he said in a low, steely tone, before storming out.

Edward hurried through the main square of Lilliput. Everywhere he looked, he saw reminders of Gulliver's influence. Gulliver's face appeared on billboards. Gulliver's name appeared on restaurants. People were even starting to dress like Gulliver, wearing stretched-out T-shirts and baggy pants. Edward shivered with revulsion, his fury deepening with every step.

Later that night a solitary boat, manned by a shadowy figure in a dark cloak, made its way through the black waters toward the Blefuscian port. Suddenly two spotlights beamed down onto it, blinding the man at the oars—Edward.

"Speak your name!" called the Blefuscian sentry.

"General Edward Edwardian. Formerly of Lilliput."

Edward was escorted toward the shore by the sentry boat, then led to the castle for an audience with the Blefuscian ruler, King Leopold. The Blefuscian castle closely resembled that of the Lilliputians, except that instead of Lilliputian blue, the soldiers all wore red, and the banners flying from the ramparts were also red.

Edward told the king all about Gulliver.

"This giant threatens not just me, not just you, but our very way of life as Lilliputians and Blefuscians!" Edward stepped up onto a handy box, and projected his voice as though he were giving a rousing speech. "You saw the way he gathered up your ships! You heard him say he has no wish to wage war! We have been at war with each other for centuries! What will our soldiers do if they are idle! He has completely transformed Lilliput from a respectable, industrious kingdom constantly at war into a fun-loving, celebrity-mongering, Gulliver-worshipping nation of indolent loafers! And he's going to do the same to *your* land! We must stop him!"

King Leopold looked thoughtful. "And how do you suggest we accomplish such a monumental and dangerous task?"

Edward smirked. "Allow me to show you my plan, Your Majesty," he replied, stepping down from his platform. He nodded toward a servant, who hurried over, dragging a long, rolled-up piece of paper.

With great care, Edward and the servant un-
rolled the huge piece of paper, revealing that it was
the cover of the magazine that had washed ashore
along with the *Knotfersail*. A picture of a robot was
still clearly visible, along with the tagline, BUILD YOUR
OWN ROBOT! BLUEPRINTS INCLUDED!

# Chapter 13

Horatio and Princess Mary strolled together in the square.

"So what are your plans for the morrow?" the princess asked Horatio.

Horatio eagerly started to answer, then caught himself. He shrugged. "Don't know. Just hanging," he replied, trying hard to be casual.

"Would you care to attend the Ball of the Moonlit Glen?"

"Maybe," he replied, polishing his fingernails on his sleeve and then examining them closely. "We'll see. I got a bunch of irons in the fire."

"Literally or figuratively?" asked the princess, annoyed.

"Both. I might be hanging with the blacksmith

guild down at the inn. Feel free to stop by if you want."

Some Lilliputian women walked by.

"'Sup, maidens?" Horatio called out to them.

The princess's brow furrowed. "Why are you acting like this? Have I said something to upset you?"

"No, baby. You're the bomb. It's just that I'm a gentleman merchant about town. Gotta keep my options open!"

Her eyes flashed. "Well, I am not an *option*. I am a *lady*!" And tossing her head, she stalked off.

Horatio smacked his forehead with the palm of his hand, then ran it down the side of his face. "What was I thinking—," he began, but suddenly the alarm bells rang out.

Over by the king, Jinks the servant cried, "We are under attack!"

"By sea? By land?" asked King Theodore, who had hastened out into the square to listen.

Gulliver walked over too, picking his way carefully through the streets.

"Five bells!" Horatio gasped.

"What does five bells mean?" Gulliver asked.

The princess had hurried back to stand at her mother's side. "Flooding?" she mused.

"Riots?" suggested the queen.

"Garbage pickup?" ventured Jinks.

"There have *never* been five bells!" Horatio exclaimed.

"Well, don't worry," said Gulliver confidently. "It doesn't matter how many bells are ringing. I got your backs."

Suddenly, from the distance, came a horrifying sound—a *creeeeak-creeeeak thunk-thunk* that shook the ground. A swell of Lilliputians flooded into the streets, their eyes wild with fear.

And then something rose over the hill as it climbed higher and higher up the ridge.

When it got to the top, it stood towering over the town, over the buildings, over the palace. It stood eye-to-eye with Gulliver.

It was shaped like a man, made of wood and metal, and its internal workings moved by a series of weights and pulleys. If one were tall enough to peer inside the head—which only Gulliver was— one could see that in the center of this mechanical device stood Edward, controlling the ropes, levers, and pulleys with newfound expertise, motivated by anger and vengeance.

Gulliver gulped, then looked down at the royal family. Gesturing with his chin toward the monstrous robot, he whispered loudly, "Edward."

"Edward, you traitor!" thundered the king. "How dare you forsake your Lilliputian brethren!"

"I only forsooked after being forsooken!" replied Edward through the crackly voice of the robot loudspeaker.

"Well," Gulliver yelled back, "the forsookingness ends now!"

The Lilliputians all cheered.

The robot spoke again, this time to the princess. "Once I defeat this beast, we shall be married. What say you to that?"

"I shall never marry *you*, traitor!" snapped the princess.

The robot swiveled toward Gulliver. "I challenge you to a duel."

"Cool, whatever," replied Gulliver. "You're on."

"Be careful!" said the queen.

"Don't worry," said Gulliver. "This thing is no match for me."

At his words, the robot suddenly transformed, growing taller and wider and more menacing than ever. It loomed over Gulliver, its expression full of vengeance.

"Uh-oh," said Gulliver. He took off running.

The robot followed him, running at a herky-jerky, yet rapid pace. It appeared to be gaining on Gulliver.

"Get that thing away from me!" shrieked Gulliver in a decidedly unheroic voice. The Lilliputians gaped at the spectacle.

As the royal family watched with growing expressions of consternation, the robot grabbed Gulliver by the back of his pants, its clawlike hand attaching to his underwear waistband and mechanically cranking up, up, up, until Gulliver dangled in the air above the Lilliputians, the victim of a giant wedgie.

"Presenting your glorious protector!" shouted Edward through the robotic loudspeaker.

The Lilliputians watched in stunned disbelief as Gulliver struggled vainly to free himself from the robot's grasp.

"I surrender! I surrender!" yelled Gulliver.

"You *can't* surrender!" the princess pointed out. "You are our glorious protector!"

"You are President Awesome!" added the king.

"And you and Captain Sparrow single-handedly

defeated the Joker and Darth Vader and . . ." The queen trailed off uncertainly.

Gulliver stopped struggling. He dangled limply above the Lilliputian crowd. "I didn't do any of those things," he admitted in a small voice. "I'm just a mail room guy."

The crowd gasped. Children began to whimper and cry.

"But you gave us your word!" said the king.

"I'm sorry. I lied," said Gulliver.

"I told you so!" said Edward the robot.

The Lilliputian crowd grew silent. They stared up at Gulliver reproachfully. Then, sadly, they turned their backs on him and slowly walked away.

A Blefuscian trumpet fanfare sounded, and a cavalry brigade trotted into the town square, horse hooves clopping, red flags flapping in the breeze. King Leopold trotted up and maneuvered his horse to stand next to the robot. Then he turned toward the princess, who cowered in fear.

"Do not kidnap me!" she said in a small voice.

"Well actually, now there is no need," said Edward from up in his robot tower.

"Right," agreed King Leopold. "Because now we

rule your land! Lilliput shall now be known as New Blefuscia!"

As the Lilliputian royal family, Horatio, the towns-people, and the still-dangling Gulliver watched, the blue flags were all pulled down and replaced by New Blefuscian red flags. The king, queen, prince, and Jinks were escorted away.

Edward, in the robot voice, addressed the crowd with another speech. "The cowardly lying beast is hereby banished to the Island Where We Dare Not Go, never to return to Lilliput again!"

The Lilliputians gasped again, horror evident on their faces.

"Uh-oh," mumbled Gulliver. "This does not sound good."

Chapter 14

Gulliver awoke from a deep sleep—possibly a sleeping potion had been slipped into his drink—and found himself bobbing on a huge raft behind an armada of New Blefuscian ships. Beyond the ships he could see a dense, ominous wall of fog. "So that's the Island Where We Dare Not Go," Gulliver said to himself, trying unsuccessfully to peer through the fog bank. "I wonder if it's really as bad as it sounds."

Twang! Twang! Twang! Twang-twang-twang! The New Blefuscians cut the ropes one by one that had been towing Gulliver's raft, and their ships immediately began to turn, away from the fog bank and back toward New Blefuscia. Gulliver's raft, meanwhile, continued to head toward the fog bank, as though pulled into it by unseen currents. As soon as he entered the fog, everything around him went gray. He couldn't see beyond his own raft.

The current seemed to gather speed, and he had the odd sensation of traveling quickly but without the ability to see any landscape by which to measure his speed. He was so disoriented he had difficulty knowing how much time was passing. Had it been five minutes or two hours that he'd been in this thick gray morass? His clothes were sodden, the air thick and warm. And then almost instantly the fog bank ended. He felt the bottom of his raft skim over sand, and he was thrown forward onto a smooth, sandy beach. Turning toward the ocean, all he saw was gray. But above him and behind him on the island, the sun was shining brightly. The beach appeared to be deserted.

He spat out some sand and sat up.

"HELLOOOOOO?" he called loudly.

No one answered. He got to his feet, brushed the sand off his damp clothes, and looked around. "Well, no little people here, anyway. That's a good sign." He began trudging along the beach in one direction. After a few minutes he came to an outcropping of craggy rocks, and clambered up them. At the top of a large rock, he stopped and stared with bulging eyes.

On the beach in front of him lay a junkyard of twisted old wrecks. Battleships, airplanes, pirate ships, pieces of boats, and assorted other articles of debris littered the beach as far as the eye could see.

"So *this* is where all the missing ships and planes from the Bermuda Triangle end up!" he said, a cold stab of fear in his gut.

As he stood gaping at the chilling scene, a giant hand came down from high above him, clasped him around the middle, and dropped him into a dark pocket.

Chapter 15

Gulliver awoke and stretched. Half-asleep, he thought he was back in Lilliput in his dream house. Shuffling into the bathroom, he turned on the water in the sink. It didn't work. Grumbling a bit, he shuffled into the kitchen and tried that tap. It didn't work either. And then he remembered that he wasn't in Lilliput anymore.

With a gasp, he hurried back into the bathroom. This time he looked at his reflection in the full-length mirror. He was wearing a dress. A frilly pink dress, a little too tight for him under the arms, and *definitely* not his best color.

All of a sudden he was flooded in bright light. Looking up, he realized the entire roof of the house had opened and been flipped backward on its hinge.

Then it all came back to him: This was not a real house. It was a dollhouse.

And *he* was the doll.

A giant little girl peered down into the house at him, frowning. She wore a crown on her head. And she was in a bad mood. In fact, she had been in a bad mood from the moment she picked him up from the beach.

"ARGGGH!" she growled.

"Uh . . . hello, little giant girl," said Gulliver with a weak smile. "Please don't smoosh me."

She grunted and scooped him up with one hand. With the other, she shoved a giant plastic baby bottle into his mouth. He tried to spit it out, but she grunted forcefully and shoved it back in again.

"Gmoo-gmoo ghrr-ghrr," he garbled.

Then the girl—was she a princess? Gulliver wondered—flopped him down on the changing table and began to change his diaper.

"Oh, now, hey!" he said, desperately trying to sit back up.

She shoved him back down again and turned him onto his side, holding up a hand as though she was going to whack his backside.

"Okay! Okay! Goo goo goo ga ga ga!" he yelled enthusiastically.

She lifted him off the table and plunked him down into a chair in the kitchen of the dollhouse. He was sitting at a table with three other creatures the same size as he was: a stuffed rabbit, a boy doll with plastic hair and bendable legs and arms, and a motionless guy wearing head-to-toe pilot gear and a visored helmet covering his face.

"Mmm," he said dully, lifting an empty plastic cup to his lips. His tea party companions did not move. And this made the giant girl very mad, so she grabbed the stuffed bunny, turned, and after a few seconds, wheeled back around and plonked the bunny back in its chair—without its head!

"Oh! Yum! Delicious!" Gulliver suddenly yelled. "Best fake tea ever!"

At that moment there was a knock at the door, and the giant girl's father poked his head into the bedroom.

"Grrrh! Garrrrrrumph!" he growled at his daughter, then reached in a hairy arm to flip off the light switch.

The girl grunted and climbed into her big

canopy bed. Soon she was snoring loudly.

Relieved that he was free of the girl for at least several hours, Gulliver stared around the table at the headless bunny, the doll, and the pilot. "So," he asked in a strangled tone. "How long have you guys been here?"

There was no response. Turning to the fighter pilot, Gulliver lifted up the visor on his helmet. Inside was what appeared to be a human skeleton.

"AHHHHH!" shrieked Gulliver. He ran and dove into a cardboard bed, hiding his head under the crackly pillow.

He thought about Lilliput and wished with all his heart that he were there again.

✳   ✳   ✳

Meanwhile, back in Lilliput—or New Blefuscia, as it was now called—the bell tower began ringing.

Horatio was hiding up in the branches of a tree, trying to come up with a plan to rescue the princess and the rest of her family. He listened carefully. "Gulliver has returned!" he whispered joyfully.

Up in her chambers, Princess Mary was also listening to the ringing bell.

"Gulliver!" she said breathlessly. "He's back."

Downstairs in the prison cells, the king, queen, Jinks, and Prince August poked their heads out and listened to the bells ringing.

"Gulliver!" they all said at the same time.

In the royal army barracks, Edward had heard the bells too.

"Gulliver," he snarled. He stood up and shrugged on his coat, hastily buttoning it as he hurried out the door.

A crowd of Lilliputians had already assembled around a wrecked boat on the beach as Edward hurried up. There in the sand lay the giant, safely tied down by hundreds of cables.

But it wasn't the same boat. And it wasn't the same giant.

Edward climbed up and stood where the giant could see him.

"State your name!" he thundered.

The giant, who was unable to move, blinked at Edward, apparently in a state of shock. "Darcy Silverman," she croaked.

"Of Manhattan?" Edward demanded.

These words seemed to completely unnerve the

female giant. "AHHHHHH!" she shrieked, and imme-diately fainted.

✷ ✷ ✷

Later that day, at the palace grounds, Horatio climbed down from the tree and stole across the dark courtyard, avoiding the red-clad New Blefuscian patrol guards. He stood staring up at the terrace where he knew Princess Mary must be, captive in her own chambers.

Up on the terrace, the princess was indeed pacing back and forth, lost in thought. Two patrol guards appeared at the top of her steps and she wheeled on them, eyes flashing. "Can I at *least* walk the terrace of my own *castle* in *privacy*?" she spluttered.

They retreated, and she continued her pacing. Suddenly she heard a soft rustle behind her and whirled around, thinking the guards had returned. But it was not the guards.

"Horatio!" She gasped.

"Princess!" he whispered, his face aglow with love.

"What are you doing here?" she whispered. "You could be caught and thrown into prison with the rest of my family!"

"I have come to take you away," he said. "I have secured a boat. We can leave tonight."

"No, Horatio." She put a knuckle to her mouth, her chin trembling.

"But Edward is going to force you to marry him!"

"I have no choice," she said woodenly.

"Yes you do! Remember what Gulliver said? He said . . ."

"Everything Gulliver has said is a lie!" she spat back. "And everything *you* said to me is too!" She whirled around and raced away from him, jerking open the door to her chamber and banging it closed behind her.

Horatio sighed. He knew he had to make things right. And there was only one person who could help him.

He slipped away into the darkness and headed toward the harbor.

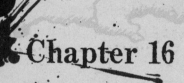

Chapter 16

The next morning Gulliver stood at the windowsill of the giant girl's bedroom. He figured she was a princess as her room looked pretty royal, especially with a throne in the corner. She seemed to be a rather lonely princess, though.

He watched through the opened window as the girl now sat on a blanket in the grass just below him, having a pretend picnic with herself. Nearby, other giant children were playing with a ball.

Just then the ball ricocheted off one of the kids' feet and rolled up to the girl. The other giant kids motioned to her to roll the ball back and join them, but she turned away.

Suddenly a familiar voice called out, "Gulliver! Hey, Gulliver!"

Gulliver turned and looked around in confusion. Then he spotted his old friend. "Horatio? How on earth did you get here!"

"There's no time to explain," said Horatio, dangling from a rope tied to the curtain rod. He caught hold of the windowsill and shimmied onto it. He looked curiously at the dress that Gulliver was wearing, but made no comment. Instead, he got right to the point. "Gulliver, you *must* return to Lilliput at once."

"Forget it, man," said Gulliver. "There's no way I can go back."

"You don't understand, Gulliver. Edward has—"

"It doesn't matter. I may be a hundred feet tall, but I'm not half the size of one of you little guys. This is where I belong, as a giant girl's baby doll—"

"Hey!" interjected Horatio impatiently. "Do you have any *idea* how *hard* it was for me to get here? I almost died, like, eight *hundred* times just walking from the perch of that windowsill over here to you! So stop talking and *listen!*"

Gulliver immediately closed his mouth.

"New Blefuscia has taken over Lilliput. Edward has captured Darcy Silverman of Manhattan!"

Gulliver blinked at him in disbelief. "What?" was all he could say. Then realization hit him like a locomotive. He remembered the series of angry messages that Darcy had left on his iPhone. "Oh no. She said she was going to get on a boat, that she had to go out and do the assignment herself, because of how I lied to her. She's here because of me."

"It isn't *all* because of you," said Horatio kindly. "But you are the only one who can fix it."

"I can't," moaned Gulliver, burying his face in his hands and revealing that his fingernails were lacquered bright red. "Don't you get it? I didn't invent basketball. My father is not Darth Vader. I'm not even the president of the United States! I was afraid to tell you guys the truth because it was so great being a big shot for the first time in my life. Truth is, I've never gotten anywhere, because I've always been afraid I'd fail. And I was right. That robot kicked my butt!"

"No, it didn't!" said Horatio. "You kicked your own butt. You ran away. You didn't even try!"

Gulliver hung his head.

"Come on, you can do this!" Horatio said encouragingly. "You saved the princess. You defeated the entire New Blefuscian navy. And you saved our king from a fiery death! We need you, Gulliver!" He pointed to Gulliver's dress. "Now take off that dress!" He pointed toward the ocean. "And let's get out of here!"

Somehow, Gulliver was convinced he had to go back to Lilliput. He tore off the dress and the diaper—he still had his shorts and T-shirt underneath—and crept into the kitchen of the dollhouse, where his tea party friends still sat around the table.

Cringing, Gulliver lifted the parachute pack off the back of the fighter pilot, coughing as a cloud of dust swirled around him. Then he crept back to the windowsill, with the pack now on his back. Horatio climbed onto Gulliver's hand, and Gulliver slipped him into his shirt pocket. He and Horatio stared down at the yard below them. To Gulliver, it was like looking down from the observation deck of the Empire State Building. To Horatio, it was like staring down into the Grand Canyon.

"How old do you think that parachute is?" Horatio asked in a trembly voice.

"Pretty old," replied Gulliver. "Maybe we should look for a really long string, just in case."

But it was too late. The door suddenly burst open, and in walked the giant girl. When she spotted

Gulliver, she let out an ear-piercing yell as she charged across the room toward him.

There was no choice but to jump.

"AHHHHHHH!"

Gulliver and Horatio yelled in unison as they fell down, down, down, the yard rushing toward them. Gulliver pulled the rip cord.

WOOOSH!

The parachute opened perfectly and they shot back up, but a stiff breeze cropped up and blew them right back in through the window of the girl's bedroom.

They zoomed past the girl, who lunged to catch them, but Gulliver swooped around her and then steered the parachute toward the open bedroom door. He and Horatio sailed out of the room and down the stairs.

As they zoomed through the house, Gulliver looked around and was surprised to see that it looked like an ordinary house. "Why, this is no *castle*," he said. "She's no *princess*. She's just a lonely girl who has no one to play with."

"Incoming!" yelled Horatio.

Gulliver looked behind them just in time to see the

girl clutching an armful of dolls, and pelting them at Gulliver one by one. The headless bunny sailed past, narrowly missing him, just as the front door swung open and the giant father appeared. Several dolls hit him squarely in the face and chest.

As the father shielded himself from the attack, Gulliver zigzagged around him and took a flying leap out of the door and into the yard. The ground rushed toward them, and they had nearly landed when they were suddenly pulled upward—by the very angry giant girl, who was holding the parachute.

"Uh-oh," said Gulliver.

The girl pulled back her huge fist, and was about to pound Gulliver to a pulp, when a ball bumped up against her foot. She looked over to see the group of kids, who looked hopefully at her. Then she turned back to Gulliver, ready to finish him off.

But Gulliver saw his chance for freedom. "Now you hold it right there, young lady!" he bellowed.

Surprised at his tone, she froze, her fist still balled up and ready to strike.

"Why spend all your time locked in your room pretending to be a princess and bossing around little helpless things?" Gulliver continued. "Is it because you're too scared to play with kids your own size? Is that it?"

The girl drooped and lowered her fist.

"It's okay," said Gulliver soothingly. "I understand. If you just play with those kids as yourself, without pretending to be a princess, I'm sure they will want to play back. Because all that matters is being big on the inside!"

Slowly, the girl took off her tiara and flung it away. Then she kicked the ball back to the kids. They smiled and waved her over to play with them.

"See?" said Gulliver. "There's nothing to be afraid of. Just be a kid! An extralarge kid!"

The girl smiled broadly.

Gulliver had one last thing to say. "Now, instead of pummeling us to a pulp, do you mind just letting us go?"

The giant girl did better than that. She actually carried Gulliver and Horatio all the way back to the beach, put them onto a raft that was still in reasonably good condition, and gave them a huge shove out to sea. As she waved good-bye from the beach, the two sailed back into the fog bank.

"Let's go save our princesses!" yelled Gulliver with a whoop.

"Yeah, about that," said Horatio uncertainly. "I attempted to use your advice with the princess, to act all standoffish as you advised. Well, Princess Mary is not my biggest fan right now."

"Yeah, Darcy doesn't like me much either," admitted Gulliver. "I'm sorry. You should never have listened to me. You should have just been yourself. Wow. I really messed everything up."

"Yeah, pretty much," agreed Horatio.

The New Blefuscian sentries paced up and down the beach that had formerly been Lilliput's. Just after they passed, Horatio's head slowly rose out of the dark waters, followed by his entire body, which kept rising higher and higher until he was completely above the sea. Beneath Horatio's feet was Gulliver's head; Gulliver rose to a standing position and, as silently as he could, Gulliver waded through the water and tiptoed toward the palace.

Down in the dank dungeons below the palace Darcy sat, chained by her arms and legs to the walls. Next door to her were the king, queen, prince, and Jinks the servant.

"More hay, she-beast?" called a New Blefuscian guard from an open trapdoor in the ceiling.

Darcy looked up, shaking away the hair that was falling over her face, her eyes flashing. "Call me 'she-beast' again and I will mess you up big-time! I'm talking smooshing you like the tiny ant that you are!"

The door hastily clanged shut. Then Darcy heard a rustling from another part of the cave. Someone her size crept up and began untying her.

"Gulliver?"

"Yeah. Hey, Darcy," Gulliver said casually. "It's so crazy to run into you here all tied up. I mean, of all the places. What's up?"

"What's up?" Darcy demanded. "What isn't up? Can we talk about the whirlpool? And how you invented basketball? And that you were married to Angelina Jolie? How do they even know who she is?"

"Well, she *is* really famous," said Gulliver lamely.

"And why does everyone keep calling me your princess?"

"You must have misheard," said Gulliver. "No one does that."

"I see you've returned for your princess," called the king from the next cell.

"See! Right there!" said Darcy. "He just called me your princess!"

"That's just what they call ladies here," said Gulliver.

"If you wish to speak privately with your one true love, we will cover our ears," called the queen.

"One true love? You told them I'm your one true *love*?"

"Okay, is this a bad time to tell you about the crush I've had on you for the past five years?" asked Gulliver.

"This would be the worst time ever."

"That's what I thought," said Gulliver.

"You know what?" said Darcy. "Never mind the past right now. We have got to get out of here. If we make a break for it, we can make it to your boat and get the heck out of here."

Gulliver's eyes lit up at the idea of running away with Darcy, just the two of them, alone in a boat. And then a resolute expression appeared on his face. He shook his head. "Look, Darcy, I know this is crazy and I'd love to run to the boat and get out of here. But these people are depending on me."

"Gulliver," said Darcy, as though speaking to a small child, "you work in the mail room."

"Not today I don't!" said Gulliver.

As Darcy watched openmouthed, Gulliver turned and ripped the door off her cell. Then he strode over to the cell next door and ripped the door off that one, too, freeing the royal family. Stooping down, he tore their chains from the wall, then held out his palm for them to step onto. He raised them up so that he could speak to them face-to-face. "If it's all right with you, I'd like to be your glorious protector again," he said.

"How can we believe anything you say, Gulliver?" asked the king sadly.

"Because my word is my bond for real this time! I promise!" Gulliver replied. "If I don't kick Edward's butt, it'll be because he's much stronger than me—not because I didn't try."

King Theodore turned to Jinks. "Send word to the New Blefuscians. Tell them our protector has returned and that he challenges Edward to a duel!"

Chapter 17

The sun was high in the sky outside the royal palace. Lilliputians and New Blefuscians lined both sides of the grand boulevard, a sea of red and blue. In a special booth sat Princess Mary and Darcy. Wearing a long princess gown and a conical princess hat, Darcy looked every bit a princess as Mary.

At one end of the boulevard stood Gulliver, dressed in ill-fitting armor hastily fashioned by Horatio at his blacksmith shop. At the other end, facing Gulliver, stood Edward's robot. Gulliver could see Edward inside the robot's head, working the controls.

Edward maneuvered the robotic head so that it faced Princess Mary. "I duel for your honor," he said, manipulating the robot into a creaky bow.

"You duel for no one's honor save your own

pomposity," replied the princess, turning away from him.

Gulliver bowed toward Darcy. "For your honor," he said loudly. Then, in a quieter voice, he whispered to her, "Could you curtsy, maybe? It's the custom around here."

Darcy curtsied awkwardly. "You need serious psychiatric help!" she hissed.

"I shall take that under advisement, my lady," Gulliver replied.

"Why are you speaking like Robin Hood?" Darcy demanded.

Before he could answer, a drumroll sounded. The robot and Gulliver squared off.

"This is ridiculous," scoffed Darcy to the princess.

"Gulliver fights to the death for your honor. Here, that's considered quite romantic," said the princess.

Darcy's mouth fell open. She looked at Gulliver as though for the first time. Her face softened as she watched the robot begin marching toward Gulliver. "Wait," said Darcy. "Did you say, 'to the *death*'?"

Gulliver watched the robot approach, and fear crept into his face. He turned, cowering from the approaching metal contraption. As he bent over, shielding his face with his arms, the waistband of his underwear became visible—a wedgie waiting to happen. Edward clearly had the same thought. Advancing the robot, he moved toward Gulliver and extended a robotic arm. A claw shot out, grabbed the top of Gulliver's underwear, and pulled up.

But Gulliver remained standing on the ground! The robotic arm held a piece of underwear, but not Gulliver. He whirled around to face the robot. "Tear-aways!" he declared triumphantly. The crowd cheered.

"The duel is on!" said the queen, clasping her hands with excitement.

Gulliver advanced on the robot and threw a punch.

ZZZZZZZZZZZZZZ!

"Ow! What was *that*?" yelped Gulliver, nursing his fist.

Edward laughed. "I've made some electrical improvements to my creation. Shocking, isn't it?"

Gulliver looked inside the control area where Edward was standing. Behind Edward, Gulliver could see his own iPhone, which had been jimmied open, electric wires coming out of it every which way. Evidently Edward had managed to harness electrical energy from the iPhone to power the robot and give it the ability to administer shocks. Despite his growing apprehension about the duel, Gulliver had to concede that Edward's technical improvements were pretty ingenious. These Lilliputians really *were* good engineers. Gulliver turned and took off at a full sprint.

The robot chased him through the city. Every time it got within reach, Edward advanced a robotic arm to touch Gulliver, shocking him painfully.

"Ow! Ow! Ow! Ow!" yelled Gulliver as he ran.

Back at the palace, Darcy stood up, flinging away her silly princess hat. "Hey! That's not fair! He's cheating! I have to help Gulliver!"

The princess looked shocked. "But that's not lady-like!" she said.

"Where I come from," said Darcy, "women don't let the men fight our battles for us. He could get hurt."

The princess smiled. "So, you're 'into' him?" she asked, crooking her fingers to make air quotes.

"What?" asked Darcy, startled. "No. I was just saying, well, I'm just worried, is all." She bit her lip and looked at Gulliver getting chased by the robot.

Horatio was also watching Gulliver with growing

consternation. Finally he leaped over the railing and began chasing after them. "Fear not, Gulliver!" he called. "I'm on my way!" As he raced past a corner of the castle, he nearly careered into Prince August.

"You'll never get to him in time," said the prince. "But I think I can help!"

"You?" panted Horatio. "How? Do you have a weapon?"

"The greatest weapon of all!" said the prince. "Acting!"

Moments later, two New Blefuscian soldiers who were guarding Edward's horse in the royal stables looked up to see a rather short, very young man in a New Blefuscian soldier uniform approach. He held Horatio by the elbow, as though Horatio had his hands tied behind his back.

"I am taking this prisoner to the stocks," said Prince August, lowering his chin to his chest and trying to pitch his voice an octave lower than it usually was. "I will need that horse."

"This is General Edward's horse," said the guard, looking him up and down suspiciously. "Who are you?"

"How dare you question me!" replied the prince.

"I am the greatest general in all of New Blefuscia!"

"You are too young to be a general," the other guard pointed out.

Quickly realizing his disguise wasn't working, Prince August went to plan B and kicked the first soldier in the shin. The other soldier quickly advanced toward the prince, who screamed for help. "Horatio! Horaaaaatio!"

Horatio stepped up from behind the advancing soldier and clocked him over the head with a handy piece of wood he'd found on the ground. Then he did the same to the other soldier, who'd been hopping around nursing his sore shin. The two soldiers fell to the ground, senseless.

"Nice teamwork!" said the prince, and he and Horatio fist-bumped. Horatio grabbed the horse's reins and swung up into the saddle. Off he went.

Meanwhile Gulliver and the Edward-powered robot had made their way to the steps of Gulliver's house. They crashed through the front door, Gulliver still trying to avoid being shocked by the robot's arm. He ran around the kitchen island, picking up pots, pans, spoons, teakettles—everything in sight—and flinging them at the robot, but nothing stopped it.

He raced into the living room, only to be shocked and sent reeling backward through the picture window where, with a splintering crash, he landed on his back in the front yard.

Inside the robot's head, Edward was loving every minute. Every time Edward swung a fist, the robot copied Edward's action and swung a fist at Gulliver.

Gulliver, on his back, scrambled backward, trying to escape the shocks and punches, but the robot was stronger. He felt himself losing the fight. He would not save the Lilliputians, or Darcy, or . . .

Suddenly Horatio came galloping up on Edward's horse. He rode up alongside the robot and threw a grappling hook upward, where it affixed to the robot's leg. Then he leaped off his horse and pulled himself up, up, up, and climbed all the way into the robot's head. He discovered Edward, working the controls, boxing with his own fists, which controlled those of the robot —which were busy pummeling Gulliver.

Horatio quietly walked up to Edward and tapped him on the shoulder. "How about we make this a fair fight?" he said. He wound up, then POW! He landed an uppercut on Edward's jaw. As Edward staggered backward, his eyes fluttering, Horatio grabbed the wires leading to the iPhone and began to rip them out.

"What are you doing?" yelled Edward.

Sparks showered down from inside the robot as Edward tried to stop Horatio from dismantling his creation. But he was no match for the muscular blacksmith. Every move Edward made, flailing and staggering around, still dazed from the punch, was mimicked by the robot itself.

Gulliver, still on the ground, watched as the robot swung and staggered around. He stood up and peered in, and saw Edward and Horatio locked in combat.

"Yeah, Horatio!" he yelled encouragingly.

One of the robot's arms flailed out and smacked Gulliver on the side of the head. But there was no accompanying electric shock. Horatio had dismantled the technology. Gulliver joined in and helped overpower the robot, with Edward inside. "Thanks, Horatio!" called Gulliver. "I'll take him from here!"

Horatio gave Gulliver the thumbs-up and, while Edward was struggling with working the robot controls to fight Gulliver, vaulted out of the control room and climbed down the robot, leaping onto a nearby balcony to safety. Gulliver continued to fight.

They struggled back and forth, moving this way and that, back toward the center of town. Then the robot landed a bruising punch, knocking Gulliver backward. He fell with a crash to the ground, right in front of the royal family and Darcy.

"Ha!" yelled Edward. "Some protector! Looks like I've defeated you once again! Edward Edwardian is the greatest lamebrain in all the land!"

Gulliver, who was lying groggily on the ground, spotted the golden basketball that had ornamented the wall that he had built. It must have broken off during their scuffle and had rolled here. He picked it up. He held it in his hand and set his feet into position, his eye squarely on his target. Concentrating, he took the shot . . . and the ball flew through the air in a perfect arc, descending toward the robot, right into the eye opening, and . . .

BAM! The ball knocked Edward out cold.

The robot teetered as the crowd below screamed and scattered. It began to fall, slowly at first, and then with increasing speed. . . .

CRASH! The robot fell motionless to the ground.

"DENIIIIIIED!" yelled King Theodore, remembering the trash talk Gulliver had taught him. He clasped his palms together and pumped them above his head as he danced a victory dance.

Horatio and the princess ran into each other's arms.

"Horatio!" thundered the king.

Horatio froze and turned toward the king.

"Do you realize what you have done?" shouted the king. Then his voice softened. "You have committed a valiant act! You helped Gulliver defeat the robot! I hereby give you permission to court my daughter!"

The crowd cheered. Suddenly everyone went silent. The king had leaped to his feet and was pointing at Prince August, his face beet red with rage.

"How dare you wear that uniform!" he shouted at his son, who was still wearing the red uniform of a New Blefuscian soldier.

"Wait, Sire!" called Horatio, breaking off from his embrace of the princess. "It's not what you think! Prince August was helping me! He helped save Gulliver!"

"How did you do this?" the king demanded of the prince.

The prince grinned. "Acting, Father!" he said.

Meanwhile, Gulliver and Darcy were standing next to each other, apart from the rest of the crowd and unsure of what to say. Gulliver broke the awkward silence.

"I plagiarized that stuff because I didn't think you would ever go out with a guy from the mail room. I'm so sorry and I'll never do that again and when we get back to our dimension do you want to maybe go out for coffee or something?" He braced himself for her rejection.

Darcy stared at him for a moment. Then she said, "You just defeated a giant robot in my honor. What do you think?"

Before Gulliver could register the happiness he felt at these words, so long imagined in his dreams, they heard a terrified scream.

Edward, with a large purple bruise on his forehead, was standing behind the princess, holding a long, shiny sword at her throat. "I have kidnapped the princess," he croaked. "Gulliver surrenders, or she dies!"

The crowd gasped. Gulliver and Horatio froze. Everyone stared at the crazed man holding the princess.

And then Princess Mary did a nifty twist in Edward's grasp, wrenching herself free and at the same time punching him. Edward slipped senseless to the ground.

"Oy," the princess said, rubbing her knuckles. "Enough with the kidnappings already!"

She and Horatio rushed back into each other's arms and embraced. So did King Theodore and the queen. Even Gulliver and Darcy hugged each other.

While everyone was embracing, the New Blefuscian king motioned to his men to quietly tiptoe away. But King Theodore saw and pulled out his sword. And the Lilliputian soldiers did the same.

"King Leopold!" shouted King Theodore. "You have waged war on Lilliput for the last time! I condemn you and all the New Blefuscians to death!"

Gulliver gently broke his embrace with Darcy and stepped forward. "Hey!" he said. "What is it with you guys and all your talk about wars and stocks and executions? Like, why all this war? I mean, why war? What is the point of . . . war? What is it good for?"

The no longer "New" Blefuscians and the Lilliputians looked at one another as though for the first time. Then they looked at all the chaos that they had created around them.

Finally, with resolve, the two kings faced each other . . . and shook hands.

Chapter 18

Gulliver and Darcy were ready to leave. The Lilliputian and Blefuscian people all stood together, ready to see them off. The two royal families, finally allies rather than enemies, stood together, dressed in their best finery. King Theodore spoke first.

"Lemuel Gulliver and his princess Darcy Silverman, we shall miss you greatly. We know you must return to your land. To celebrate, we have renamed the lands of Lilliput and Blefuscia . . . Lillafuscia!"

King Leopold's smile faded. He turned to King Theodore. "I believe we actually renamed our lands Blefilliput."

"No," said King Theodore. "We agreed it would be Lillafuscia."

The two kings reached for their swords. Gulliver

cleared his throat. "Can't you just agree to disagree?" he asked heartily.

This seemed to make sense to the two kings.

"Let us agree to disagree," said King Theodore.

"Yes. It is official," said King Leopold. "We shall agree to disagree."

Gulliver turned toward Horatio. "Horayshe," he said. "You're my best bud. I'm really proud of you and all you've done."

"Thank you, Gulliver. I shall miss you."

"And I you," said Gulliver, dabbing at the corner of his eye and sniffing hard.

Horatio put out his fist. Gulliver bumped it with his own, his eyes welling up.

"Ohmigod," said Darcy. "You're crying."

"Am not," said Gulliver.

"You're totally crying," insisted Darcy.

He and Darcy climbed aboard the *Knotfersail*.

"Three cannon blasts for Lemuel Gulliver!" shouted King Theodore. "The man who is truly the greatest lamebrain in all the land!"

"Lamebrain! Lamebrain! Lamebrain!" chanted the crowd.

The boat chugged away from shore.

"Lamebrain?" asked Darcy.

Gulliver kept smiling and waving. "Just act like it's awesome," he said out of the corner of his mouth.

As they chugged past the last part of Lilliput, they saw Edward, toiling away in the hot sun, dismantling the wall that Edward had forced Gulliver to build. They waved cheerfully at him. He waved angrily back.

And soon the *Knotfersail* approached the giant whirlpool. . . .

Epilogue

Six months later . . .

A taxi pulled up in front of the *New York Tribune* building, and Gulliver jumped out. He headed into the lobby, where he pushed the up elevator button.

Upstairs, Gulliver hung up his things before settling down at his desk. The nameplate on the desk read LEMUEL GULLIVER: TRAVEL WRITER. His fingers tapped away at his keyboard as the creak of the mail cart approached. He stopped typing and looked up.

"Hey, Dan!" Gulliver called out heartily. "Still in charge of the mail room, huh? Holding down the fort?"

Dan glumly handed over Gulliver's mail.

"Who's your friend?" asked Gulliver, gesturing to the young man standing behind Dan.

"I'm Mark," said the young man, holding out his

hand toward Gulliver. "Just the new guy in the mail room."

"*Just* the new guy in the mail room?" repeated Gulliver. "The mail room is where it's *at*. All the greats start there. You treating my mail chariot well?"

"Yes, sir," said Mark.

"Keep the dream alive, Mark," said Gulliver. "There are no small jobs. Only small people. Tiny, tiny, tiny little people."

He bumped fists with Mark, who looked a bit confused as he walked out the door and trailed after Dan.

A while later Darcy bounced into Gulliver's office and came around his desk to plant a kiss on his lips.

Then she dropped the day's *Tribune* on his desk. "Fresh off the presses!" she said, then asked, "How was Papua New Guinea?"

"Hot. Sticky. But wildly exciting. Here's my story," he answered, grabbing a stack of papers from the printer and handing them over.

She took the article and smiled at him. "The most wildly exciting thing you've ever done?" she asked with surprise.

"Well," Gulliver replied with a laugh, "maybe the *second* most wildly exciting thing."

"Can I buy you lunch?" Darcy asked.

"Of course you can, my fair princess," said Gulliver, offering her his arm as they walked out.

The *Tribune* on Gulliver's desk lay open to the travel section. Opposite Darcy's picture was one of Gulliver, heading up his own column. It was entitled "Gulliver's Travels."